ASCLEPIUS

CHRISTOPHER M. RUTLEDGE

Adam

Thanks for your support!

Enjoy Adam!

Book and cover design by Christopher M. Rutledge

Cover illustration by Nuwbia Design Studio

Edited by Tammy Rutledge

ISBN: 978-1795731928

Library of Congress Control Number: 2018909960

Printed in the United States of America

First Printing, 2019

Kindle Direct Publishing

"To Wellness"

Dr. Geoffrey Chance Du Bois

CONTENTS

1

IMHOTEP

Various herb plants along several shelves in small planters line the entire wall of the kitchen. A recessed grow-light glares from the ceiling above them, as a large water bug crawls along one of the shelves. It's a warm humid morning just before dawn in Atlanta, Georgia. The room is silent with the exception of a slight buzz from the grow-light and the occasional clanking of a lone fork against a plate.

Dr. Geoffrey Chance Du Bois, African-American man in his late 30s, has breakfast alone in his kitchen. He's dressed in slacks, vest, and a neatly tied bowtie. His face is covered with a full beard and mustache.

Dr. Du Bois dejectedly nibbles on a nova lox bagel and a hard-boiled egg. He stares at a framed portrait of his ex-wife Judith; and two young daughters Mary, and Elizabeth. The photograph sits directly in front of him as though he's dining with them.

A white lab coat lies folded across a chair next to him; beneath it, a modest briefcase. Anubis, his full-grown black Doberman Pinscher, looks up at the table wagging his stump of a tail.

A patient sits in the waiting room. He's a middle-aged African-American man wearing brown slacks and a matching aged homburg hat. He casually flips through the pages of a health magazine. Brenda, a young nurse, opens the door to the waiting room and leans inside, "Willie Ollins?" He looks up and closes the magazine, "Right here."

Dr. Du Bois, in his lab coat and bowtie with tight-fitting glasses, sits in a task chair typing on his laptop. He raises a finger in the air. "Be with you in one moment, Mr. Ollins." Shortly after, he rolls his chair toward Mr. Ollins.

"We're going to start you on these new supplements and a new meal plan." Dr. Du Bois hands him his prescription. Mr. Ollins grabs the slip of paper and beams as he looks at Dr. Du Bois. "I can't thank you enough Dr. Du Bois. For this new...life and lifestyle." Dr. Du Bois smiles compassionately.

Mr. Ollins continues, "My cancer's been in remission since I started treatment with you, I'm one of the few people in my family to live past 55, and I NEVER felt better!" Dr. Du Bois smiles very widely.

"Words likes this Mr. Ollins, they make me glad to get out of bed every morning...before dusk." They both laugh. Mr. Ollins looks at the slip of paper and struggles to pronounce one of the names.

"Astaaa—"

"Astaxanthin. This one is most important actually. Very powerful antioxidant."

Dr. Du Bois places his hand on Mr. Ollins' shoulder. He looks him in the eyes solicitously. "E-mail me with any questions whatsoever." Mr. Ollins nods affirmatively.

"See me again in three weeks, OK?" Mr. Ollins heads toward the exit door from the exam room. "Thank you, Dr. Du Bois!"

Dr. Du Bois rolls his task chair back to his desk. Without looking up, he raises a finger and says, "...And only wild caught salmon. No substitutes!" Mr. Ollins laughs as he leaves the exam room.

Moments later, the door to his exam room creaks open. Dr. Du Bois has his back to the door as he writes notes. "What can I do for you, Brenda?"

"Nope. It's me. Gotta sec?" Dr. Simon Mathers, a forty-something Caucasian-American man, walks in carrying a briefcase. Dr. Du Bois spins his task chair around, excited.

"Simon! Thought you left for vacation already." Dr. Du Bois stands to greet him with a handshake.

"Taking off now, actually."

"Anywhere exciting?"

"Gonna hang around Atlanta for a few days, then off to the BVI!"

"BVI. Awesome!

"Yup!"

"Tell Sharon hello, and congrats on her new job."

"You got it. Thanks!"

As Dr. Mathers is about to exit the room he turns around. "Hold down the fort, brother!" Dr. Du Bois laughs. He and Dr. Mathers have known each other for close to twenty years and have worked together for about five of those years, so they have a pretty good friendship and report outside of work.

The medical office has closed for the day. Dr. Du Bois cruises down the I-75 highway through downtown Atlanta in a clean 1983 240D series Mercedes Benz. The metallic gold paint is in mint condition. National Public Radio (NPR) plays on his radio. The NPR Host says, "Some people think those missing natural medicine doctors is part of some government conspiracy."

Dr. Du Bois shakes his head at the assertion, then mumbles to himself, "Tomfoolery." He immediately turns off the radio, uttering, "Complete nonsense."

He arrives at the Atlanta Civic Center. His modest briefcase in tow, Dr. Du Bois walks down the hallway and appears to be somewhat of a local celebrity. Several patrons acknowledge and greet him as he approaches a set of double doors. He returns greetings and smiles as he walks through the doors to the auditorium.

The auditorium is filled with people of several races, largely African-American. Dr. Du Bois stands at a podium below a large yellow banner that reads, "10th Annual Alternative Medicine Symposium by Dr. Geoffrey Chance Du Bois, ND". Dr. Du Bois looks intently at the crowd.

"Thank you all for coming." He looks up at the banner. "Ten years? Someone correct that." The audience laughs and applauds.

"For those of you that are new; this is an open forum, not a speech, so please feel free to interject and engage openly and freely."

Almost instantly, a quirky geeky African-American teenager sitting on the front row, raises his hand. Dr. Du Bois laughs, "We have a question already." He points at him to speak. "Go ahead young man."

The teenager stands and awkwardly peers around the room. He wears an Atlanta Falcons baseball cap hung low over his head. Dr. Du Bois squints, giving him an inquisitive look to make out the identity of the teenager. "Justin?" he asks. The teenager raises his cap a little, revealing himself a bit more.

"Yep, I'm back again."

"Welcome back, Justin!"

"I followed your career for a while. Started a blog about it actually!" His name is Justin Jakehorne and he operates a natural health blog and follows several noted alternative medicine doctors, primarily Dr. Du Bois' developments in alternative medicine focusing on alternative cancer treatments.

Dr. Du Bois smiles proudly as he rubs his beard, "Impressive." Justin continues, "So my question is regarding..." He hesitates and appears nervous. Dr. Du Bois smiles, "It's OK. Ignore the large crowd." Justin takes a deep breath, then continues, "…Regarding the recent deaths and disappearances of alternative medicine doctors. What are your thoughts on that? Is it coincidence, or…"

A hush falls over the crowd. Justin sits down abruptly. Dr. Du Bois laughs it off, "…Or a government conspiracy? No, I don't believe those rumors of the small few that share them. Albeit an odd coincidence, but no, I do not believe in conspiracy theories, particularly those." Justin reluctantly nods. Dr. Du Bois clears his throat, then continues.

"There's been a lot of advancements in alternative medicine over recent years, and proven success rates of older practices." Dr. Du Bois holds up a pamphlet. "Underneath your seats, you'll each find one of these." As the audience reaches under their seats, he laughs.

"Sorry, I'm not Oprah, just pamphlets." The audience laughs and proceeds to reach under their seats.

"Garlic and honey. I swallow a diced clove every morning myself. Make those staples of your diet along with foods high in antioxidants. Your plate should contain an assortment of natural colors, primarily darker; purples, reds, oranges, and of course greens."

"Avoid vices such as smoking, alcohol, and those slow killers such as sugar, flour, and processed foods, and you can live to be one hundred." Dr. Du Bois looks around the room, pointing at the audience. "The best health care, is PREVENTATIVE health care! When we age it is said that we are destined for disease as a direct result of our age. That's a lie!" The audience reacts from his passion. "Most diseases that fall upon us in old age are a direct result of how we treated our bodies in youth. The human body is a temple, and if we respect and revere this temple throughout our lives, it will become a place of refuge when we need it most." The audience applauds.

He holds up a book. "My latest book, 'Lifestyles of the Living Gods,' goes into much greater detail. To sweeten the deal, pun intended, a small portion of the proceeds from the sales of this book is donated to the Honeybee Conservancy." He nods proudly. "One in every three bites of food we eat is pollinated by honeybees." Most of the audience looks surprised by this figure.

At the conclusion of the symposium, Dr. Du Bois sits at a table greeting audience members and signing copies of his book.

Justin stands near the front of the line. When he reaches Dr. Du Bois, he excitedly grabs a signed copy of the book, holds it up, then takes a selfie with Dr. Du Bois. They both smile widely. Justin shuffles with his phone as he uploads it to Instagram almost immediately. "Almost forgot," says Justin, as he hands him a business card. "Here's the new blog!"

Dr. Du Bois smiles and nods affirmatively. He tucks the card in his vest pocket. "You have a lot of positive energy, Justin. Continue to live your purpose, son." Justin smiles proudly. He's raised by a single mother and although Dr. Du Bois doesn't exceed him in age by many years, Justin senses a paternal energy from him. Justin views Dr. Du Bois as a positive African-American male role model, a mentor, and takes comfort in his approval.

The symposium has ended and Dr. Du Bois heads home. As he cruises down the highway, he reaches over to the passenger seat and grabs his cellphone. He pulls out Justin's card, peeks at it, then pulls up his blog on his phone. Dr. Du Bois looks up and sees his highway exit quickly approaching. He nearly misses the exit, slamming on his brakes and swerving abruptly to exit the highway. He skids onto the exit ramp a nervous wreck.

He throws his cellphone on the passenger seat. "It's not a smartphone if you do DUMB SHIT with it, Geoffrey!"

As he glimpses in his rearview mirror, he notices a car behind him. It exits abruptly as well. The car follows him down the access road. Dr. Du Bois ignores the car for the moment and continues driving.

Dr. Du Bois makes a turn at a corner, then looks in his rearview mirror. The car still follows behind him. He makes another turn, yet the car still follows, turning behind him.

As Dr. Du Bois peers at the mysterious vehicle in his side mirror, his car chimes. He looks down at his fuel gauge. The fuel level is low. He pounds the console with his fist. "Dammit!"

He looks in his rearview mirror and slows down as he approaches his affluent neighborhood in Cascade Heights.

The mysterious vehicle makes a turn on a side street. Dr. Du Bois breathes a sigh of relief.

His Mercedes Benz speeds into the garage. The overhead door closes immediately behind it. Dr. Du Bois' garage is obsessively neat. Bright white epoxy coating covers the floor. He parks next to a 55-gallon drum labeled, "Biodiesel." The drum is equipped with a fueling pump. Several empty cooking oil containers and empty five-gallon buckets sit neatly stacked next to the drum. He pumps a few gallons into his car.

Dr. Du Bois dines alone in his kitchen enjoying a glass of red wine and a pescatarian meal. The portrait of his ex-wife and daughters sits at the corner of the table. A flank steak steams on a plate. Dr. Du Bois tests the temperature of the steak with his finger. He looks down at his companion, Anubis, then tosses the flank steak into his dog bowl.

"Fish for me. Grass-fed beef for you." He licks his fingers of the beef fat residue. "Sometimes, I miss you."

He walks to the refrigerator. As he reaches in to grab his bottle of red wine, he scans the shelves for a snack. He looks at an orange, but grabs a cookie instead.

Later that evening, Dr. Du Bois and Anubis sit on the couch. He relaxes with his glass of wine reading a book, "The Herndons: An Atlanta Family." A wooden tongue depressor serves as his bookmark. The position of the bookmark indicates he's about halfway through.

The minimalist living room has a pronounced oil painting of Imhotep on the east wall, with the inscription, "Father of Medicine." A life-sized statue of Asclepius stands in the corner of the room. Instead of a rod, his hand rests on a real sword, sitting inside a coiled serpent serving as its sheath.

Anubis' ears perk up like horns. He stares at the front door. "What's up, boy?" Dr. Du Bois looks at the front door, then looks at Anubis. He points at the front door. "I fed you steak! Go investigate!" Anubis runs to the front door.

A sound on the rear patio, off the living room alerts Anubis. The bushes ruffle. Anubis darts back to the patio door, barking fervently. The noise quiets. Anubis' fervent barks eventually fade.

"Probably just another deer," says Dr. Du Bois. He taps the front edge of the couch seat, "Come here, boy." Anubis trots over and lies on the floor near the couch. Dr. Du Bois continues to read his book. An eerie silence blankets the house; the chorus of crickets and night creatures outside, more pronounced.

Suddenly, silenced gunshots zip through the patio door, poking lethal holes into the couch. They miss Dr. Du Bois by inches. He leaps to the floor. "Anubis! Get down!"

Instead, Anubis sprints from the living room and darts through the kitchen. He dives through the dog door, heading for the assailant. Dr. Du Bois lies on the living room floor, panicked. He sneaks to grab his cellphone from the bullet-riddled couch.

Vicious growls from Anubis emanate through the patio door. Dr. Du Bois looks at the patio door in terror as he calls 911 for help. Outside the patio door, the sound of a struggle ensues. The growls get more aggressive, followed by a loud crash. There's dead silence.

He yells into the cellphone in a muffled whisper, "Someone's trying to kill me! They're shooting through my door!" He crawls on his elbows to his Asclepius statue, then pulls the sword from the statue's hands. The sound of the steel sword pulling from the stone casting is that of a knight unsheathing a sword.

Dr. Du Bois takes cover again. The phone still pressed to his ear. "Who's THEY? I don't know! Murderers I suppose?" He listens for a moment, "In Cascade Heights…1313 Audubon Court." He nods frantically. "Yes, near Cascade Road and Benjamin Mays Drive."

A few moments later, Anubis casually strolls back into the living room. Blood drips from his fangs and muzzle. He sits on guard next to Dr. Du Bois.

2

CORUSCATION OF LIGHT

Atlanta Police Detective, Kyle Mercer stands in Dr. Du Bois' kitchen. He holds a small notepad and pen, chewing his gum slowly and deliberately. He's a middle-aged Caucasian-American man with a rotund shape; and a native Georgian evidenced by the heavy drawl of an accent. Dr. Du Bois sits at the kitchen table, distressed. He holds his head in his hands.

Dr. Du Bois raises his head from his hands, "…And no shell casings? How is that even possible? He fired at least seven bullets at me!"

"I mean…it could mean—"

"—That this was a hired professional?" asks Dr. Du Bois with a sarcastic tone.

Detective Mercer is quiet for a moment. Dr. Du Bois' expression flips to anxious fear.

"No?"

"We'll put our best folks on this one."

"Really? I don't have a description of him...or her, God forbid."

Dr. Du Bois points at Detective Mercer's notepad. "And you didn't write down ONE THING I said." He shakes his head in disbelief.

"I've been doing this a while, doctor." Detective Mercer slowly flips the cover closed on his empty notepad. "Plus, we got the video from your security camera on this."

Detective Mercer holds up a flash drive. Dr. Du Bois looks at the flash drive, then looks at him. He appears to be losing faith. The detective continues. "Even though it was dark outside, we got people that could fix those sorts of things."

Detective Mercer peels a weathered business card from his wallet and lays it on the kitchen table. Dr. Du Bois looks down at it.

"If you see or hear anything out of the ordinary, you call me. Directly!" Dr. Du Bois stands up to shake Detective Mercer's hand as he leaves.

"We got a vehicle in your subdivision watching your house for the night." As Detective Mercer stands in the doorway he catches glimpse of the herb plants along the wall of the kitchen. He squints for a moment, then shakes his head.

Dr. Du Bois sits in the kitchen. He stares at his empty wine glass. He gets up and looks out of his window. There is no sign of a police car watching his home. He walks into the living room. He looks at his bullet-riddled couch, the small specks of glass still sparkling on the floor, then the plywood over his patio door.

The alarm indicator "dings" repeatedly, as the passenger doors of Dr. Du Bois' vehicle sit open inside his garage. He tosses a garment bag into the backseat. It's so heavily packed that it resembles a body bag. Anubis hops into the front seat. Dr. Du Bois slams both doors shut. He quickly hops into the driver's seat, then slams his door shut.

He speeds down the driveway from his garage. He looks in the rearview mirror at his house as it gets smaller and smaller, finally disappearing into the night.

The hotel door is locked with both the deadbolt and security latch. Hotel furniture is stacked blockading the front door. Anubis lies, coiled like a serpent, nearby.

Dr. Du Bois reaches into the garment bag lying on his bed, and pulls out the sword. He sits at the desk peering at his laptop; he is focused. His glasses tight on his face. The sword shimmers nearby.

He pulls up the Meharry Medical College website. He chooses an option to "search for alumni." He scrolls and browses several profiles. He stares at one profile in particular. The name reads, "Ola Fulani".

He clicks on her name.

In a large empty parking lot of a shopping mall, a lone car sits at the rear of the lot near a dumpster. The silhouette of a driver, no passengers, is seen through the window. A black garbage bag, ripped open, lines the driver seat. A first aid kit lies on the passenger seat next to him.

He pulls out a pair of bandage scissors and proceeds to cut open his bloody pants leg. He grimaces as he cuts down the outer seam of his pants. He pulls the separated pant leg apart, exposing three large dog bite wounds on the side of his leg, just below the knee.

Slowly reaching into the first aid kit, he pulls out a large bottle of iodine. He douses it on his injury as he breathes profusely through his gritted teeth. The antiseptic burns his scarred tissue. Fumbling around in the first aid kit, he pulls out a small syringe in a plastic wrapper.

It reads "Lidocaine" on the side of the vial. He tears off the wrapper, bites off the cap on the needle, takes a few deep breaths, then stabs his leg with the syringe just below the wounds. He grinds his teeth and grunts, but does not yell, as he injects the numbing agent.

Pausing for a moment from his self-surgery, he lights a cigarette with his butane lighter. As the cigarette hangs from his mouth, he grabs a wound stitch kit, then proceeds to stitch up his wounded flesh as his cigarette ashes over. A few painstaking minutes later, he bands gauze around his leg, then finishes it off with medical tape.

He sits up and stares into the rearview mirror. Smoke rises as a pair of steely blue eyes stare back at him.

3

GUARDIAN OF THE SCALES

The Soul Vegetarian Restaurant on Atlanta's Westside is fairly busy and nearly filled to capacity. Dr. Du Bois sits at a table, very rigid in posture. Across from him sits Dr. Ola Fulani. She's biracial (African-American and Caucasian-American) and about the same in age as Dr. Du Bois. Contrasted by his rigidness, Dr. Fulani is very relaxed with an energetic smile that brightens their proximity. She wears a bright yellow dress with a matching carnation tucked into her large curly afro.

"So nice to reconnect with you, Geoffrey!"

"Yeah. It's been quite some time now. You, you look great, Ola." Stuttering as he nervously adjusts his glasses. He nervously thinks to himself. "She's a doctor, and of all things, you comment on her physical appearance. Sexist!"

"Likewise!" Dr. Fulani looks at his vest. "You've always been such an old soul. You wear that vest well, sir."

"Thanks." His blushed smile is no longer suppressed.

"So, what made you reach out?" She asks, as she takes a sip of her green tea.

"About that." Dr. Du Bois clears his throat. "I'm sure you've heard the news about our...fallen comrades?"

"God yes! That's so awful!" She leans in and whispers, "I think they're related." She nods affirmatively, driving her point home. Dr. Du Bois expresses surprise at her assertion. He looks around the room, then leans forward meeting her halfway across the table. "Initially, I didn't feed into the rumors, Ola, but..." Dr. Du Bois looks over his shoulder, then whispers, "...Last night, someone tried to kill me!"

"What?!? Are you serious?"

Dr. Du Bois looks her directly in the eyes. His eyes partially glazed over. He remains silent for a moment.

"Oh my God! Are you OK, Geoffrey?"

"No, but I will be, and I want to make sure you are as well."

"Thank you."

The waitress returns to their table. Without looking up, Dr. Du Bois puts up a finger. The waitress expresses her discontentment with the arrogant gesture, then walks off.

He leans back into his seat, then points at Dr. Fulani. "You've always been...progressive, forward-thinking. That's part of the reason I've reached out to you."

"Militant! Go ahead and say it." They both laugh. She continues. "Not as much as I used to be though, since I've had my little mini me."

"Oh, I didn't know you were married."

"I'm not."

"I'm sorry."

Dr. Du Bois shifts with a nervous awkwardness. Dr. Fulani laughs uncomfortably. She holds her green tea to her mouth as she stares over the cup. "It's OK. I'm focused on my career right now." She takes a sip.

"Understood."

He takes another paranoid look around the room, then leans in a bit. "So, what I devise, is we do our own investigation."

"I've already started actually," says Dr. Fulani confidently.

"Share it with me."

Dr. Du Bois takes a sip of his coffee and nibbles a bagel. They both lean in closer. She breaks down her investigation thus far.

"So, two of the deaths were ruled suicides." Dr. Fulani pulls up a photo on her phone as she continues, "But I've spoken with the families and NEITHER believes this to be the case."

Dr. Du Bois looks at her intensely. "Very interesting."

She hands the phone to him. He looks at an autopsy report. As he pinches the screen to zoom in on the image, Dr. Fulani points at the phone. "That's for the doctor found in her car underwater in New Jersey. Ruled a suicide."

He zooms in on a diagram of the body on the autopsy report. There are two dark circles denoted on the back of her head.

He looks up abruptly. "These are consistent with gunshot wounds." Dr. Fulani nods affirmatively, "Yup." He hands the phone back to her, then slowly leans back in his seat. He rubs his beard in contemplation.

Dr. Du Bois pulls out a pill vial and pops a few pills. He downs them with his water. Dr. Fulani looks at him curiously, wondering what he's taking, but remains silent.

The Atlanta Police Station servicing Zone 4, has a few patrons sitting around the lobby. Dr. Du Bois is amongst them. Legs crossed; he reads a copy of the Atlanta Journal Constitution newspaper.

A cop walks in with a young Black male in handcuffs, which catches Dr. Du Bois' attention, so he watches. He appears to be maybe twenty-something, pants sagging, and low eyes. The suspect complies as he walks inside, but he protests, "Just one lil bag of weed and I'm going to jail for that?"

The cop nods smugly, "Yup. You know that's illegal, right?" The suspect shakes his head. "This some bullshit my nigga! Mufuckas out here doing much worse than smoking weed." Dr. Du Bois shakes his head, then looks back at his newspaper.

Detective Mercer strolls out to greet.

"Doctor!"

"Detective." Toneless, Dr. Du Bois doesn't raise his eyes above the newspaper.

"Nothing new yet, unfortunately."

Dr. Du Bois slams his newspaper shut. "I was nearly murdered! I didn't think this would be so slow moving."

"We're working on it round the clock, doctor."

"I mean, it looks like you're spending more resources to catch this kid for smoking a reefer than finding a potential hired gunman," he says as he points at the young man in handcuffs.

Detective Mercer pops two pieces of gum in his mouth. He looks at the suspect, then looks at Dr. Du Bois as he nods.

"Any luck making out the fellow in the video?" asks Dr. Du Bois.

"You know. I meant to contact you. Do you have any copies?"

Dr. Du Bois pauses in thought briefly. He looks at the detective skeptically now.

"No, why?"

"Unfortunately, one of our newer officers we're training misplaced that thingamajigger."

"You mean my flash drive? The 'thing' with the film footage."

"Yeah. That little booger."

Dr. Du Bois shakes his head as he laughs. "Consummate professionals you guys are."

"Sorry about that. This doesn't usually happen. We'll contact you when we know more."

Detective Mercer watches as Dr. Du Bois walks out of the station.

Officer Travis Carlyle, Caucasian-American man in his early twenties, casually strolls into the lobby as Dr. Du Bois leaves. He eats an apple with a pocket knife. Officer Carlyle looks at his boss, "Sorry bout that flash drive. I don't know where the hell that thing went." He throws a slice of the apple in his mouth. Detective Mercer looks at him.

Justin sits in his bedroom on his laptop. It resembles a hybrid of a college dorm room and a hip-hop archive. There are 90s era hip-hop albums covering many of the walls. White text fills the black computer screen as he rapidly types into the Command Prompt. A Georgia Tech pennant hangs on the wall just behind the laptop.

Debbie Jakehorne, his mother, walks into the bedroom. She's an African-American woman in her fifties, and slightly on the heavy side. Upon opening the door, Justin hastily minimizes the screen, then spins his chair around. Debbie notices the covert gesture and quickly covers her face.

"Oh, I'm sorry. Didn't know you were—"

"Ma, I knew you were visiting. I'm not…never mind." He shakes his head, blushed. "What's up?"

"Finally started reading your…blog."

"Oh yeah." Justin is more enthusiastic about their conversation now.

"Yes, and I've given our chats some thought."

"About?"

"About changing my lifestyle, eating habits."

"That's dope, Ma!"

"Yep, and I stopped at the DeKalb Farmer's Market. I'll get dinner going so I can head out before too late."

"Cool." Justin spins his chair back around and goes back to work on his laptop.

Debbie smiles at him as she leaves, admiring his commitment and diligence.

The sword glistens on the corner of the hotel room desk. Furnishings still stacked high against the door, Dr. Du Bois stares at his laptop screen reading an article on Justin's blog. The article title reads "Alternative Medicine Murders? by Justin J."

As he reads the article he focuses on a few keywords, "possible connection; US Food & Drug Administration; pharmaceuticals."

Dr. Du Bois closes the website and shakes his head. He takes a drink of wine.

He opens a folder on his computer, then searches for files on his hard drive. He types the words "security camera" in the search box.

A list of video files populates. He sorts them by date, then scrolls to the most recently dated video file labeled "patio camera." He double-clicks to open it.

He watches it intently as he sips his wine. The video starts out a complete black mass.

"Dammit!" Dr. Du Bois slaps the table.

Suddenly, the video illuminates and the patio is visible. The motion sensor light on his patio has activated in the video.

A dark figure skulks from the bushes. He sneaks onto the patio carrying a pistol. He wears a black military-grade uniform with a black baseball cap. The dark figure looks directly into the hidden camera, unaware that it exists. He fires a single silenced round, disabling the patio floodlamp below the hidden camera. BIP! Dr. Du Bois jumps when the shot is fired. The video goes black.

His cellphone rings. He looks at the black laptop screen, then stares at his phone for a moment. It's Dr. Fulani calling.

"Ola?" Dr. Du Bois looks at his watch. It's past 12AM.

"Geoffrey, you won't BELIEVE this shit!"

"What happened? You OK?" Dr. Du Bois pulls the sword closer on his desk.

"No! Somebody ransacked my fucking house."

"What?" He now holds the sword in his hand, as he peers around the room.

"Yeah. They were looking for something."

"Perhaps YOU! Are you safe?"

"Yes, thank you. I'm staying...with some family."

"I'm sorry to get you involved in this. I feel partly responsible." Anubis wakes up. Dr. Du Bois looks at him, a bit alarmed.

"No don't blame yourself for this, Geoffrey. They would've come for me eventually. You know...since I fit the victim profile."

Dr. Du Bois nods in agreement. "What can I do for you?"

"Don't worry about me. I'll take care of myself. They only succeeded in driving me to commit to this, one hundred percent now!"

Dr. Du Bois facetiously raises a fist in the air. He nervously quips to break the tension.

"Power to the people."

Dr. Fulani gives a faint chuckle, knowing this is paying tribute to her culturally conscious views and militancy while attending Meharry Medical College.

"Hey, I want you to meet someone tomorrow, Ola."

"OK. I'll see how much of this I can get sorted out first."

Dr. Du Bois saves the security video file to a flash drive, then shuts down his laptop.

Computer and tech magazines cover the coffee table in Justin's tiny apartment. Amidst the chaos, sits a neatly arranged fruit bowl, at the center of the table.

Electronic devices and computer equipment are scattered about the room; several monitors, a laptop, a server, a desktop PC, and various external hard drives. His custom-built PC has a see-through glass wall showing the motherboard and other inner workings. It's illuminated with a bright red light.

A large flat screen television hangs on one wall. Justin's laptop is displayed on the television screen. He sits on the couch wearing a Nas t-shirt, basketball shorts, and flip flops. Dr. Du Bois and Dr. Fulani flank him on each side of the couch, gazing at the screen.

"Can't believe that detective misplaced key evidence in a potential homicide," complains Dr. Du Bois.

On the television screen, the security video feed is paused at the frame where the dark figure first shows his face on camera. Justin ticks forward frame by frame as Dr. Fulani and Dr. Du Bois carry their conversation in the background.

"Misplaced? Yeah, OK. If you had less melanin, I'm sure it wouldn't be *misplaced*," claims Dr. Fulani.

Justin nods in agreement as he continues to peer at the screen, "Totally, fam."

Dr. Fulani shakes her head in disappointment. "Our circle of trust is shrinking by the day."

Justin frantically points at the screen.

"Ay! Yo! Check it out!" The doctors look closer. Justin continues. "See that tattoo on his neck?"

"Yeah, on his throat," replies Dr. Du Bois.

He zooms in on the neck of the dark figure. The tattoo resembles a blue and gold rectangle.

"Looks like…" Justin thinks for a moment. "The Ukrainian flag?"

Dr. Du Bois nods affirmatively.

"Yes, it does."

Justin zooms out from the tattoo image, showing the whole face of the dark figure. He adjusts the gamma correction and lightens the image a bit. The face is slowly revealed, partially. He moves the cursor, clicks, and selects the face of the dark figure.

He drags and drops it onto an icon on his desktop. The app begins to scan the face. It runs it against a database. Several faces flash across the screen.

Dr. Fulani gives him a tense inquisitive look. "OK. So, what do you do for a living exactly, Justin?" He hesitates for a moment, then chuckles. Dr. Du Bois looks at him curiously.

"IT, but when night falls, I hack."

Dr. Fulani shifts uncomfortably. Justin continues working on his laptop as he continues.

"Don't be alarmed though. My dark web activity; it's all for social justice. I'm a HACKtivist." Dr. Fulani smiles and pats Justin on the arm. "That's so awesome, Justin!"

The application runs for several minutes in the background. Several faces continue to flash across the screen. Justin yawns. "This app may take a while. A lot of faces to scan."

Dr. Du Bois' phone rings. Without looking at the screen, he answers on the first ring, "Dr. Du Bois." He casually grabs an orange from the fruit bowl.

"I've been trying to reach you." It's his nurse, Brenda.

"Oh, my hotel has horrible reception. Everything OK?"

Brenda hesitates for a moment. "Simon."

"What about Simon?"

"He's dead."

"What?" He drops the orange. It rolls across the floor. "No!"

Brenda starts to cry. "He's dead. He was involved in a car accident. His car was found in the Chattahoochee River a few days ago."

"Everything's going to be all right, Brenda." Justin and Dr. Fulani look at Dr. Du Bois, concerned.

"Take. Take, the rest of the day off." Dr. Du Bois hangs up the phone slowly. Justin and Dr. Fulani continue to look at Dr. Du Bois. He dolefully looks back at them.

"A colleague of mine, Dr. Simon Mathers. Found his car in the Chattahoochee."

Dr. Fulani shakes her head. She walks over and rubs Dr. Du Bois' shoulder. "I'm sorry, Geoffrey." He's silent for a moment. Dr. Fulani continues to gently rub his shoulder as he looks glumly down at the floor, pensive.

"If I could get my hands on that autopsy report…" He whispers.

Justin looks up from his laptop. "I can probably get that for you." Dr. Du Bois looks at him curiously. Justin nods affirmatively. "Yeah. Soon as I wrap this up." Dr. Du Bois pats him on the shoulder.

"Where's your restroom?" asks Dr. Du Bois.

"Down on the left."

As he walks down the hallway to the bathroom he catches glimpse of a small figurine on a table. He looks closer. It's the Egyptian deity, Anubis. It sits on a small black box that resembles a small sarcophagus. A pyramid sits adjacent. He smiles as he enters the bathroom.

Dr. Fulani has spotted Justin's Nas t-shirt and a conversation is underway about hip-hop.

"So, he's your favorite Rapper, even today?" she asks.

"No doubt. Second only to Pac...now he the GOAT! I mean I respect the evolution of hip-hop, but I like that old school vibe."

"Impressive." Dr. Fulani laughs.

"How so?"

"I mean, you were just a baby when Tupac and Nas came out, but I like that." She nods in approval.

"My cousin's a Rapper actually."

"Really? Who?"

"Country Boy."

Dr. Fulani laughs. "The Trap King?"

"Yep. The Trap King himself."

Justin reaches under the coffee table and pulls out a CD, then lays it on the table. It's the Trap King album. Country Boy sits on a straw throne holding a red cup, donning a tilted crown; resembling the famed Biggie Smalls painting. Fitting since he's similar in appearance and stature.

"...interesting." Dr. Fulani smiles.

Dr. Du Bois returns to the living room.

"I like your statue. Anubis, that's my dog's name!"

"No kidding?"

"No kidding."

"Maybe when all this is over, I'll gift it to you."

PING! The computer application finishes up the facial recognition scanning. The sound alerts them, so they reposition themselves on the couch staring at the flat screen television.

A name appears on the screen with a short description. The doctors read the screen aloud together.

"Viktor Kalashnik." They look at each other, then continue. "Sergeant with the...Ukrainian Special Operations Force." The headshot shows a man with a chiseled jawline with blonde hair and blue eyes.

"Hunting down lowly alternative medicine doctors, with an assassin?" Dr. Du Bois shakes his head.

"Sounds very deliberate," replies Dr. Fulani.

Dr. Du Bois rubs his beard in brief thought. He grabs an apple from the fruit bowl. "Calculated, yes."

"Dang. I knew something was up!" Justin continues, excited. "This is getting more interesting by the minute. Gonna brew some coffee. See what else I can dig up."

"Thanks Justin."

"No worries."

"I can't thank you enough for your work here today."

Justin nods as he continues to type away on his laptop.

The doctors leave Justin's house and head to the car. Dr. Du Bois opens the car door for Dr.

Fulani. "Such the perfect gentleman, Geoffrey. Thank you." Dr. Du Bois smiles.

They sit in the car, idling in Justin's driveway. Dr. Du Bois appears a bit dejected.

"I don't know what to make of all of this. It's getting more intriguing by the minute, however."

"We're gonna figure it out, Geoffrey. We're both fairly intelligent. Let's use that to our advantage."

Dr. Du Bois nods, then pops a few pills. Dr. Fulani looks at him curiously.

4

PEACE IS DANGEROUS

Scratching the surface of the next morning, Justin sits slumped over his computer. The flat screen television on the wall, filled with a profusion of windows from various websites, lights the dark room. His headphones blare old school hip-hop. Vibing to the beat and lyrics of "Thieves In The Night" by Black Star, he's focused.

He takes a sip from his coffee cup. It's empty. He looks at the coffee pot. It's also empty. "Shit." He shakes his head, but continues his grind.

Justin hones in on an article on Madilyn Hardwick with the US Food and Drug

Administration. He clicks a picture of her to enlarge it. "Madilyn Hardwick," he mumbles to himself. Justin selects the text in the article with his cursor, then copies and pastes it into a blank document. He types a few additional notes in the document, then saves it.

Quick staccato taps on the keys is the only sound in the room.

A few hours later and close to dawn, Justin's bedroom is pitch black. He tosses and turns in bed. He can't sleep, so he rolls from the bed. He sits on the edge of the bed for a moment, sluggish. He squints at the time on his alarm clock. It reads 3:57AM. He steps into his slippers.

Using the walls to brace himself in his sleep-induced state, Justin staggers toward his bathroom. As he stumbles to the bathroom, he hears a sound. It appears to come from his living room.

He freezes and looks around, but doesn't see or hear anything. He shrugs, then continues to the bathroom. As he reaches the threshold of the bathroom entrance, Viktor Kalashnik suddenly leaps out of the darkness of the hallway.

He quickly wraps a leather belt around Justin's neck. He pulls it tight. Justin struggles as Viktor chokes the life out of him. Justin helplessly kicks his feet as he tries to pry the belt from his neck.

Viktor pulls Justin into the dark bathroom. "No…" Justin attempts to scream. He disappears into the darkness of the bathroom.

At about high noon, Dr. Du Bois and Dr. Fulani sit in the parking lot at Justin's apartment. Dr. Du Bois holds his cellphone pressed between his ear and shoulder. He's calling Justin's cellphone. It continues to ring. He hangs up the phone, then shakes his head.

"Went to voicemail again. His car's here though."

"Poor kid. I'm sure he stayed up all night. He's probably sleeping."

Dr. Du Bois looks at his watch. "He specified a 12PM meeting." He shrugs, then exits the vehicle with Dr. Fulani.

He knocks on the door. Dr. Fulani stands behind him. When Dr. Du Bois knocks, the door creaks open. The doctors look at each other. They enter slowly and cautiously. Everything looks the same as the day before.

"Justin? You home, sweetie?" asks Dr. Fulani with maternal warmth. Dr. Du Bois probes the room, peculiarly.

He slowly walks toward the bathroom. The light is on. The door is cracked. The exhaust fan hums. "Justin? You in there, buddy?" Dr. Du Bois knocks. There is no answer, so he enters cautiously.

Justin's body hangs from the shower-head with a leather belt around his neck. He is naked. His face is blue. A bottle of sexual lubricant and an adult magazine nearby. "Oh God, no!" Dr. Du Bois yells.

Dr. Fulani runs towards the bathroom. "What is it?" She attempts to walk inside. Dr. Du Bois grabs her in his arms.

They sit in Justin's living room. Dr. Fulani weeps heavily. Dr. Du Bois cries as he comforts her in his arms.

"He didn't do this to himself!" Dr. Fulani yells in a teary voice.

"I know. We have to get out of here."

Dr. Fulani nods in agreement. Dr. Du Bois offers her a handkerchief.

He continues. "I mean out of town, far away."

"He worked so hard for us," cries Dr. Fulani.

Dr. Du Bois looks up. Enlightened. "Wait. You're absolutely right." They peer around the room. Dr. Fulani wipes her tears, then grabs a slip of paper from the table. She uses it to conceal her fingerprints as she pulls open drawers. Dr. Du Bois looks around the room.

Dr. Fulani opens a drawer. She spots a Guy Fawkes mask in the back of the drawer. It startles her initially. She smiles, then closes it slowly. Dr. Du Bois spots Justin's laptop bag on the floor. He swiftly walks over, then frantically grabs it.

"Dammit." It's empty. He throws the bag on the floor. "Should've known."

The bag slides across the floor and hits the table holding the Anubis figurine.

The figurine rattles on the table, then slows to a pronounced stop. Dr. Du Bois focuses on the figurine. He walks up to it. He picks it up. The top comes off of the base over the black box. There's a secret compartment. Dr. Du Bois reaches inside. He pulls out a gold flash drive.

He runs into the living room raising the flash drive in the air.

"Got it!!"

"Now, let's call the cops."

Several policemen stand around the living room. Dr. Fulani and Dr. Du Bois sit on the couch. Detective Mercer stands in front of them with a notepad. He takes a few notes. Officer Carlyle stands behind Detective Mercer with a contemptuous look.

"Strange seeing you here, doctor," says Detective Mercer as he looks up from his notepad.

"He was a friend!!" Dr. Du Bois yells, frustrated.

Detective Mercer's smile transforms to a scowl. He looks up from his scribbling of notes.

"We got both of your fingerprints all over this place," claims Detective Mercer. He chews his gum intensely.

Dr. Fulani fires back. "We told you he's a friend. We visit him often, officer!"

Detective Mercer points at her with his pen, "Detective." Then points at his badge. Dr. Du Bois shifts uncomfortably.

She continues. "Actually, are we being detained, detective?"

"No."

Dr. Fulani picks up her purse. "Are we under arrest, detective?"

"No."

Dr. Fulani adjusts her dress. "Since we're free to go, we'll be leaving now. Let's go, Geoffrey." Dr. Du Bois follows behind as they leave. He appears surprised.

Officer Carlyle observes the exchange. "You gonna just let them leave?" Detective Mercer gives Officer Carlyle a condescending look. "Of course. It's their legal right!"

As they walk to the car, Dr. Du Bois looks at Dr. Fulani. She doesn't see him, but he looks at her with a bit of unforeseen fascination.

Dr. Du Bois backs carefully out of Justin's parking lot.

"I think I'm going to exercise my second amendment right to a firearm."

Dr. Fulani turns to look at him directly. "You don't own a gun?"

"You do?"

"Below the Mason-Dixon line, who doesn't?"

"Hmmm."

"I'm self-reliant. So, I carry a nine."

"I see."

Dr. Du Bois looks at her. She continues. "Plus, I'm not only fighting for me." Dr. Fulani scrolls through images on her phone. She hands it to Dr. Du Bois.

He looks at an image of Dr. Fulani with her young daughter. "She's beautiful! What's her name?" Dr. Fulani smiles. "Afeni."

One of the police vehicles from Justin's place drives past Dr. Du Bois' car. He takes a nervous look at the vehicle. It's Detective Mercer. They make eye contact as he drives by.

"I don't have time to get properly registered for a firearm unfortunately," says Dr. Du Bois as he watches the police cruiser speed ahead.

"Whoever ransacked my house, stole mine."

Dr. Du Bois pauses in thought for a moment. "Wait! I have a cousin. Down in south Atlanta."
Dr. Fulani looks surprised. "The south side?"

5

ONCE BROWNSVILLE

Vintage vehicles with elaborate paint jobs and large rims are parked throughout a lot of an apartment complex on Atlanta's south side. Dr. Du Bois and Dr. Fulani sit in their car taking in the surroundings.

Silhouettes of shadowy characters stand around the parking lot under plumes of marijuana smoke. They boldly gawk at the out of place visitors.

"You OK?" asks Dr. Fulani. He nods affirmatively. "Yeah, of course. Let's go." They exit the vehicle.

Dr. Du Bois walks with a fast pace towards an apartment door, nearly leaving Dr. Fulani. He looks back at her. "By the way his name is Todd, but he goes by..." Dr. Du Bois shakes his head. "...Skrill." Dr. Fulani laughs.

He knocks on the door. Skrill opens the door almost immediately as he carefully clinches a blunt between his index finger and thumb. He wears two lavish gold chains draping over a black tank-top; his arms, covered in tattoos. Loud trap music booms from the house with a large cloud of marijuana smoke.

"That was quick," says Dr. Du Bois. Skrill ignores him for the moment and stares at Dr. Fulani from toe to head, then back down to her toes. He responds to Dr. Du Bois while still marveling at Dr. Fulani.

"My folk called me. Said they saw a nigga in a bowtie walking up. Thought you was my PO..." Skrill starts to laugh.

"...Or trying to sell me some fucking BEAN pies!" Skrill let's off a very hard laugh. It slowly evolves into a flurry of "weed" coughs from the blunt he's smoking. Dr. Fulani smiles and giggles. Dr. Du Bois, not amused, doesn't find it funny.

"What's good, queen? I'm Skrill." He extends his hand to Dr. Fulani for a handshake. She reaches her hand out, but he pulls her hand towards him, then kisses it softly. "Nice to meet you, Skrill. I'm Ola."

Skrill waves a hand gesture to the shadowy characters out front, signaling that everything is OK. "Ay! We good folk!" He flicks away the blunt roach outside, then closes the door.

They sit around Skrill's living room. The small apartment is filled with drug money improvements suited for a young adult; a large flat screen television nearly covering an entire wall, several game systems, and a few items accentuating his southern flair...bright colored crocodile leather couches.

Two of his comrades, a young thug with locks and a brawny female thug, lounge deep into the couch with low eyes. The young thug's phone chimes. Skrill looks at his crew.

"Ay. Give us a minute folk." The crew slowly rises from the couch. The young thug looks at a message on his phone as he strolls out of the room. He looks at Skrill.

"Ay, B said hit him up."

"What he want?"

"Prolly weed. I don't know!"

"I'm getting up with him tomorrow anyway."

The young thug shrugs and continues out of the room.

"Leave that blunt though!" Like a lobster pincer, Skrill reaches out his pinched fingers for it.

He sinks into his crocodile couch and takes a pull from the blunt. Dr. Du Bois fans away the smoke.

"So, what brought you out here, cuz? Don't hear from you that much."

"Yeah. We need to change that. That's a subject for another time though." Skrill nods in agreement.

"Well, Todd...I mean Skrill." He hesitates for a moment. "I need a gun." Skrill laughs and coughs.

"Gun? Nigga, this Georgia. Why don't you buy one from the sto'? You ain't got no felonies!" Skrill sits up on the couch. "Wait, do you?"

"Of course not! I just don't have the time to register properly, and..."

"And what? Talk to me folk."

"...And someone's trying to kill me!" Skrill stands up and paces around the room.

"What! You? For what?" Skrill cocks his gun. Dr. Fulani jumps.

"Cuz, you know I know some people." He takes a pull from the blunt. "Shit, I AM those people!"

Dr. Du Bois shakes his head. "It's a rabbit hole so far. I'll have to give the full story later, but he's a trained assassin." Skrill flops down on the couch with his mouth open, speechless.

Dr. Fulani chimes in. "It's true. They're after me too. Have you seen the news about the alternative medicine doctors that have turned up missing?"

He nods affirmatively as he takes a long hard pull from the blunt. He inhales deeply and responds in a raspy voice. "Me and my ole lady was talking about that the other day." He takes another hard pull, then points at his blunt. "Forgot that's what you do, cuz. With the herbs and shit."

Skrill reaches under the table and pulls out an immaculate 9mm Glock handgun. He slams it on the table.

"This here. It's brand new. No bodies on it." Dr. Du Bois' eyes widen at the notion. "Well, that's a huge plus."

"Hold seventeen shots so you got a big ummm…" Skrill snaps his finger to trigger his memory. "Margin of terror."

"You mean margin of error," says Dr. Du Bois.

"Nah, margin of terror!" He smiles deviously.

Skrill grabs the gun and demonstrates. He grips the gun firmly with both hands. Points it at the wall. He looks through the gun sights down the barrel. "Just get him in these sights folk. Then keep squeezing, till that muthafucka drop."

Dr. Du Bois shakes his head. "Thank you, for that, crude lesson."

Skrill directs his attention to Dr. Fulani. "And please take care of this goddess. You got this glow and this energy; I can feel that shit." Dr. Fulani smiles. "Thank you, Skrill."

"Self-preservation. Stay alive! And call me if you need me cuz." Skrill daps Dr. Du Bois and brings him in for a half-armed hug, patting him on the back. Dr. Du Bois awkwardly obliges.

BOOM! BOOM! BOOM! Three loud knocks on Skrill's door. Everyone in the room jumps.

"POLICE! OPEN THE FUCKING DOOR!"

Skrill puts his guns under the couch. Dr. Du Bois hands him his gun frantically.

BOOM! The Atlanta Police kick the door in.

Atlanta Police Officers with guns pointed, storm the living room. They yell commands. "Get on the fucking floor! Everybody! Floor! NOW!"

They all drop to the floor. Skrill puts his hands behind his head protesting the raid. "Fuck ya'll think ya'll is? Red Dogs? Them muthafuckas been gone. I ain't even did shit!" One of the Atlanta Police Officers kicks him in the side several times. "Shut the fuck up with all that lip!"

The doctors lie down obliging and grow more nervous. Dr. Du Bois looks at Skrill worried, knowing how the outcome can turn out for him. He gives a pleading gesture whispering, "shhhh…please."

Moments later, Skrill and his crew sit on the curb in handcuffs. Dr. Du Bois and Dr. Fulani stand near the police car with an Older Detective. He smokes a pipe. Dr. Du Bois rubs his wrists. The Older Detective looks at Dr. Du Bois' bowtie and Dr. Fulani in her dress. "Just be careful about the company you keep. You're free to go, sir and ma'am," says the Older Detective. Smiling warmly, "Thank you Detective," says Dr. Fulani.

Dr. Du Bois drives his car with Dr. Fulani riding shotgun. He pops a few pills as he drives down the road. Dr. Fulani observes curiously. Still wondering what medication he's taking.

"So, we're on the run now?" asks Dr. Fulani.

"For now." Dr. Du Bois looks at her. "Who's looking after Afeni?"

"Her father. She's staying with him. Thanks for asking."

"OK. Good. I'll stop for some cash. Get us a motel. Checked out of mine today."

"Yeah. Need to keep moving."

Dr. Fulani reaches into her purse. She pulls out the 9mm Glock from Skrill's. Dr. Du Bois' eyes widen in shock.

"What! How?"

"Well, it's brand new and I have my gun card, so if they found it, I'd be in legal possession." She shrugs, then puts it into his glove box. Dr. Du Bois is silent for a moment as he drives. He looks at Dr. Fulani, inquisitively.

    She continues, "I slid it in my purse while on the floor." Dr. Du Bois is silent for a moment, then looks at Dr. Fulani. "Who are you exactly?" Dr. Fulani smiles.

6

HIPPOCRATIC OATH BREAKER

The Anubis figurine, black box, and flash drive from Justin's apartment sits on a nightstand in a hotel room. Dr. Du Bois and Dr. Fulani sit on opposite beds. The nightstand separates them. He reads a newspaper.

Dr. Fulani looks at the Anubis figurine as she reaches for a glass of water.

"Who's looking after Anubis?"

"My ex-wife."

Dr. Fulani reacts, very surprised. "You were married?"

"Why is that so hard to believe?"

Dr. Fulani looks at the full pajama set he wears awkwardly. She giggles.

"No, it's just that…I mean, you just seem so…"

Dr. Du Bois looks at her over his newspaper. "Socially recluse."

"I was going to say solemn. Solitary."

Dr. Du Bois reaches for his wallet from the nightstand. He pulls out a folded photograph. He unfolds it, then hands it to Dr. Fulani. She looks at the twice folded picture with crease marks across his ex-wife's and daughters' faces, then holds the decrepit photograph in the air. "Do better, please, sir."

Dr. Du Bois points at the photo identifying them. "My ex-wife, Judith. And these two angels are Mary and Elizabeth."

"Awww. You have a gorgeous family, Geoffrey."

"Thank you."

"Makes me miss my baby, Afeni."

"You'll see her soon." Dr. Du Bois smiles. She returns the gesture.

They look at the laptop sitting on the desk. It's closed and powered off. Next to the laptop sits a plastic container of mixed fruit and a large jug of alkaline water.

"I'm afraid to open that thing," says Dr. Du Bois.

"Why?"

"Afraid Viktor will track us from our IP address or something weird."

"Shit!" She hops off the bed and grabs the flash drive.

"What?"

"I almost forgot."

Dr. Fulani opens the laptop. She points at the keyboard. "Log on." Dr. Du Bois reluctantly sits at the desk. "When you went to the bathroom at Justin's the other day." Dr. Du Bois nods his head affirmatively.

"Justin showed me how to adjust a setting so you can't be tracked through it," she continues.

"That kid. Such a true martyr."

He hangs his head low reflecting for a moment. Dr. Fulani puts her hand on his shoulder. Her eyes water. "So sorry, Geoffrey."

He looks at her warmly and nods. "His death is another reason—"

"—His MURDER!" Dr. Fulani interjects.

"Right. Murder. His Murder is another reason we need to figure this out." Dr. Du Bois logs on to the computer. "Excuse me for a moment." He walks to the bathroom.

Dr. Fulani looks on the nightstand and sees a small toiletry bag half open. A prescription pill bottle is visible. Dr. Fulani looks at the bathroom door, then sneaks over to the bag.

She pulls out the bottle. It reads "Clonazepam." She mumbles the name under her breath, surprised. The toilet flushes. Dr. Fulani scrambles to put it back in his bag. She rushes back to the laptop. He strolls out of the bathroom. "All right. Let's see what Justin has for us."

Dr. Du Bois opens the jug of alkaline water on the desk. He pours two tall glasses.

He scrolls to an untitled document on the flash drive as he sips. He double-clicks to open it. It's a note from Justin:

Madilyn Hardwick - Deputy Commissioner for Medical Products, U.S. Food and Drug Administration. Google her. There's a possible connection to Viktor. I'm drawing cold leads. I'll research more tomorrow. Here's a link to a recent press conference for now.

Dr. Du Bois clicks the hyperlink. A video plays.

The headline along the bottom of the screen reads, "US FDA Press Conference." Madilyn Hardwick, a middle-aged Caucasian-American woman, stands behind a microphone at a podium in a blue pants suit with short dark hair. She appears very relaxed with the poise of a seasoned politician.

Her badge reads, "Deputy Commissioner for Medical Products." The US Food and Drug Administration seal is affixed to the front of the podium. Journalists from various news stations fill the room.

Madilyn engages with a journalist. "Yes. After rigorous clinical trials, Dynotriol has met FDA approval." Madilyn looks around the room inquisitively, "Anymore questions?"

Another journalist raises her pen in the air.

"Ms. Hardwick, I got one for you."

"What you got, ma'am?"

"So, what are your thoughts on the disappearances of those alternative medicine doctors?"

Madilyn quiets for a moment. "With all due respect Tina, wrong acronym. I think that's a question for the FBI...not the 'FDA'. My condolences to the families though."

The video ends. Dr. Du Bois looks at Dr. Fulani. He appears unsettled. Dr. Fulani looks at him for a response.

"What's up Geoffrey?"

"I lobbied against that drug last year, Dynotriol. The side effects are awful! They can lead to possible brain damage. I put out a white paper on it." Dr. Du Bois shakes his head.

"So, what is it? I've seen the billboards and ads plastered all over."

He sits up, excited to expound. "A very costly cognitive enhancer." Dr. Fulani appears to have a particular interest in this subject. She sits up, very attentive. "Interesting. Go on," she says. Dr. Du Bois sips his water. "The problem that I have primarily is that it falsely touts the ability to reduce the risk for brain cancer, when I've heard the contrary actually." Dr. Fulani looks off into the distance; she's silent.

Dr. Du Bois looks back at the files on the flash drive. A file name catches his attention. It's labeled, "Simon Mathers Autopsy Report." He selects the file, then hovers the mouse over it. Dr. Du Bois looks at Dr. Fulani. She rubs his shoulder.

He slowly double-clicks to open the Autopsy Report:

Cobb County Office of the Medical Examiner

Medical Examiner's Report

Name of the Deceased: Simon Mathers

Dr. Du Bois pauses for a moment, then scrolls down past the report. He scrolls to a diagram of the body. The illustration of the front of the body shows lacerations on his legs and chest. The illustration on the rear of the body shows a small black dot on the back of the head. Dr. Du Bois zooms in on the black dot.

There is a scribble mark over a handwritten note near the black dot. He zooms in attempting to make out the notes scribbled over. The note appears to have once read "possible GSW?" He looks at Dr. Fulani.

"Just like the woman in New Jersey." Dr. Du Bois shakes his head. He looks down in despair for a moment. "They killed Simon! I've known him for nearly two decades!" Dr. Fulani rubs his back. Dr. Du Bois looks at her frantically.

"Let's send a message to ALL of our colleagues. Warn them to be EXTREMELY cautious," pleads Dr. Du Bois.

"K. I'll do that now actually."

"Let them know we've found a definite connection between the murders." They both sit back for a moment processing the information.

"Just curious. What field did Simon specialize?" asks Dr. Fulani.

"Molecular virology."

"Wow."

"Yeah. Simon developed methods to kill viruses on a molecular level through natural medicine."

Dr. Du Bois is silent for a moment. Dr. Fulani asks, "What's on your mind?"

"I was just wondering, why was my murder attempt different. It wasn't covered up in any way. It was an outright assassination attempt."

"Maybe to break up the pattern?"

"Ah, interesting!"

"Or to send a message."

"Also interesting."

They're both quiet for a moment. Dr. Fulani looks at him. "So, the FDA is involved?" She shakes her head. "Our own government? Not at all surprised."

"Well, there is no proof it's the entire organization. Just appears to be Madilyn Hardwick."

"She's the Deputy Commissioner for Medical Products!"

"Yeah, UNDERNEATH the FDA Commissioner and Chief of Staff!"

Dr. Fulani defiantly shakes her head in disagreement. She appears agitated. Dr. Du Bois continues, "Had she been in that position we could possibly blame the organization at large, but she's not in charge of the FDA!"

"Damn. After all of this, you're still so naïve, Geoffrey. So naïve…sometimes dangerously!"

"No, I just like to act only on substantiated facts!"

There is tense silence for a few moments. Dr. Du Bois grabs a few pieces of fruit from the fruit bowl. He doesn't eat them. He relaxes himself with a few deep breaths, then attempts to diffuse the situation. He looks at Dr. Fulani, warmly.

"All we have are each other, right now." Dr. Fulani looks at him, then reluctantly nods.

"I'm sorry about your friends, Geoffrey. I know you're under a lot of stress."

"Yes, you as well, Ola. This is all so stressful."

"Most importantly, let's find out who she's working with. Expose them all."

"I agree, and sorry for being naïve…and a complete jackass." Dr. Fulani smiles at him, admiring his humility and his self-awareness regarding his ingenuous behavior. She's noticed his credulous approach since the beginning of their investigation, but she sees an arch in his disposition.

"What are you smiling about?" He asks with a wide grin of his own.

"You know, this is a bit off topic, but I've been meaning to ask you something for a long time now."

Dr. Du Bois looks at her curiously.

"Go ahead. Shoot."

"Are you related to—"

"—William Edward Burghardt Du Bois?" He laughs. "You're just NOW asking me that?" He inquires as he continues to laugh.

"I mean, I heard rumors at Meharry, but didn't know if they were true."

"You have far more restraint than others. Most ask me as soon as they hear my last name." He rubs his beard. "Well, unfortunately I'm not. I have a high level of respect for him though!" He adjusts his posture, sitting up more rigidly.

"Admire his philosophy and accomplishments. Read many of his books."

"Double consciousness." Dr. Fulani throws out.

"Ah yes. Souls of Black Folk."

"Still applies today."

"Indeed!"

"Two souls…" Dr. Du Bois continues.

"Two thoughts…"

"Two unreconciled strivings…" They say in unison, citing a passage from the book. They have a small moment when they gaze at each other. They laugh it off.

Dr. Fulani looks at him. "I'm more of a Garvey girl though." She nods.

"No surprise there." He laughs.

Dr. Du Bois stares off into the distance. "We have some French ancestry. I lived in France for a bit as a kid as well. Just outside Paris." Dr. Du Bois sits back cogitative for a moment. He ruminates about his lunches as a kid at La Madeleine in Paris. This triggers him out of his daydream.

He sits up and looks at Madilyn Hardwick's picture on the laptop screen. He leans in toward the laptop and types "Madilyn Hardwick, FDA office" in the Google search box. The search results yield an address, "20 North Michigan Avenue, Chicago, IL".

Dr. Du Bois looks at Dr. Fulani inquisitively.

She responds by nodding affirmatively, "Yeah. Let's do this shit."

Squinting from the bright sun as he walks down the steps from the police precinct, Skrill carries a small plastic bag containing his wallet, shoe strings, and other small personal belongings.

There's a car waiting for him at the curb, a blue 1970 Ford Mustang. The motor idles with a muffled rumble.

He hops into the passenger seat and leans over to kiss Tatiana, his girlfriend, sitting in the driver's seat. Tatiana's African-American and in her mid-twenties. She wears blue hair with green highlights and looks straight forward with a scowl as the muscle car growls down the road.

"I'm still mad," she complains.

"What?"

"What? You don't need to be in jail, Negro."

Skrill shakes his head, then turns to the back seat. His ten-year-old son, Tarajee, sits in the backseat, quiet. Skrill pulls his gold chains from the plastic bag and puts them on as he talks to his son. "What you quiet for?" His son's still quiet. Skrill looks at Tatiana.

"What he quiet for?"

"Ask him."

"Ay lil man. Talk to me," probes Skrill. His son looks at him. His big innocent eyes are watery. Skrill looks at Tatiana and gestures with his fingers to his mouth for something to smoke. She points to the ashtray. He flames up the blunt, takes a hit, then turns back to his son.

"What's the matter, T?"

"I got caught with something," he whispers, not actually wanting his father to hear his response.

Skrill looks at Tatiana concerned. "What he get caught with?" She hands him a plastic bag. It's filled with colorful recreational prescription pills. Skrill's eyes widen and his mouth drops as he fumbles with the pills looking at the assortment.

"He got caught with this?!"

Skrill turns to his son. "You got caught with this?" As he shakes the bag of pills. "Oh, we real cool now huh? Bringing drugs to school." Tarajee starts to cry.

"Don't cry now! What you doing with this shit?!?"

"It's just candy."

Skrill looks at Tatiana with an expression fused with anger, shock, and heartbreak. His high now blown, he throws the blunt out of the window as they speed down I-85.

He sits back in the seat processing the situation. His cellphone rings. The caller reads, "Country Boy".

"What up B?"

Skrill nods his head as though Country Boy can see him. "Yep I'm out! Heading home now." He listens for a bit. "OK folk. Yeah, I'll roll with you."

He hangs up the phone. They speed down the highway. He stares out of the window at an airplane flying overhead with its landing gear released.

Passengers scurry along the brightly lit, white marble tile corridor of the Hartsfield-Jackson Atlanta International Airport. The scene is interlaced with intercoms making flight related announcements. Dr. Du Bois and Dr. Fulani wait at their gate to board the plane. She reads a copy of CRWN, a natural hair magazine. He reads a copy of the Atlanta Business Chronicle.

The Gate Agent at their gate grabs the intercommunication device, "Delta Flight 1117 from Atlanta to Chicago will begin boarding shortly."

Dr. Du Bois takes a break from reading and looks around the gate area. He notices a mysterious guy watching them, peeping over a newspaper. He wears a leather Members Only jacket and driver cap. Dr. Du Bois makes eye contact, then the mysterious guy raises the paper.

He taps Dr. Fulani, then points his head in the direction of the mysterious guy, whispering, "Look. With the driver cap." She watches him for a bit. The mysterious guy tucks his newspaper under his arm, then leaves the gate area. He has no luggage. They look around the gate area. The mysterious guy has disappeared and is no longer in sight.

"That was really odd don't you think?" asks Dr. Du Bois.

"Too bad we couldn't bring that nine you got from Skrill."

"Right!"

The airplane is in flight. Dr. Du Bois reclines his seat to get some rest. The seat next to him is empty.

Dr. Fulani returns from the restroom. She slowly walks up the aisle. She glances at the various seats to the left of the aircraft looking for Dr. Du Bois and her seat. She finally spots him and just as she's about to get Dr. Du Bois' attention, she makes eye contact with the passenger seated behind them. It's the mysterious guy they saw watching them at the gate.

Dr. Fulani yells when his cold eyes meet hers. The commotion draws the attention of other passengers. Dr. Du Bois jumps out of his sleep. He looks around frantically.

"Ola! What's the matter?"

"Sorry. Sorry. Turbulence and heels don't mix."

Dr. Fulani seats herself. She discreetly points at the seat behind them. Dr. Du Bois takes a peek. He spots the mysterious guy and starts to sweat. He reaches for his carry-on bag. He rifles through it.

"Dammit! My pill bottle's in my check-in bag."

"You OK? What are you taking?" Dr. Fulani puts her hand over Dr. Du Bois'.

"Nothing. I'll be fine." Dr. Du Bois gives a faint, awkward smile.

Moments later, Dr. Fulani notices Dr. Du Bois' hand is shaking and clammy. She pushes the call button for a Flight Attendant. A blonde Flight Attendant arrives shortly after the notification.

"What can I do for you ma'am?"

"Yes. Can I have a cup of hot water please, for some tea?"

She looks at Dr. Fulani's curly afro, fascinated. "Wow! I LOVE your hair. Can I touch it?"

Dr. Fulani gives a disapproving look. "Make that two cups, and no thank you." She smiles.

Dr. Fulani pulls a small plastic bottle from her purse. Dr. Du Bois looks over curiously.

"What do you have?"

"Just a tincture. Skullcap, passionflower, kava kava...and CBD."

Dr. Du Bois smiles. "Nice! Never tried CBD though."

She snickers. "Helps me relax and sleep. I'll pour you a cup."

"Sure, I'll give it a shot."

Dr. Fulani prepares the concoctions as he watches on.

Moments later, Dr. Du Bois sleeps soundly with an empty cup in his hand. His mouth hangs open. His hand no longer shakes. Dr. Fulani looks at him, then smiles.

They arrive at the Chicago O'Hare International Airport. Dr. Du Bois and Dr. Fulani walk briskly through the massive corridor of the airport. He munches a granola bar with fervor as they pace through the airport.

"So, first thing tomorrow morning, we'll pay Madilyn's office a visit," says Dr. Du Bois.

They simultaneously look over their shoulders. There is no sign of the mysterious guy that appears to be following them.

"It's a federal building so security will be extremely tight," replies Dr. Fulani.

Dr. Du Bois takes a look over his shoulder.
"I have a plan for that."

7

BIG PHARMA

A brisk Chicago morning at a bustling café, the doctors sit across from one another. The café is located on the ground level of the federal building, which houses Madilyn's office. Dr. Du Bois, discrete with a cap pulled low on his head and shaded glasses; he sips a cup of black coffee with an open-faced nova lox bagel. Dr. Fulani, also discrete with her hair braided beneath a scarf; she sips herbal tea. They've been here since the café opened, scouting for clues and waiting for their next play. They periodically peer out of the window.

"Nova lox. I can eat this every day." Dr. Du Bois chews intensely, then continues. "Can't find good lox in Atlanta."

She nods. "Chicago's the perfect place for a true gastronome."

"Foodie, I think the millennials call it."

Dr. Fulani laughs. As she pivots in her seat, she overhears part of a cellphone conversation from a gentleman at a table nearby. An East Indian Man, late thirties, in a tailored suit sips espresso and chats, "I'll be meeting with her at noon." He takes another sip, then continues chatting, "Yes. Madilyn. At the FDA building now."

She kicks Dr. Du Bois' foot to get his attention. He's overheard the latter part of the conversation as well and stops chewing. They both listen attentively.

The East Indian Man continues his conversation. "OK. I'll call when we wrap." He grabs his espresso, then heads for the exit.

Dr. Fulani pulls out a digital camera. She checks to make sure the flash is off, then snaps several photos of him as he leaves.

"Who do you think he is, Geoffrey?"

"I have no clue. Could be legit?"

"Or not?"

Dr. Du Bois nods his head. They watch as the East Indian Man walks past the storefront glass window of the café.

"And there was nothing on Justin's flash drive about him?" Dr. Du Bois shakes his head, negatively. "No, not that I recall." Dr. Du Bois takes a sip of his black coffee.

"What time was that meeting?" asks Dr. Du Bois.

"Noon." Dr. Fulani looks at her watch. "We'll have to be careful though. If she's the one that organized the hit-list she may recognize us."

"We'll be hiding in plain sight. I doubt she thinks we're bold enough to visit."

"Or crazy enough."

A few suited patrons walk about the lobby of the federal building. Dr. Du Bois and Dr. Fulani stand in the elevator lobby holding their cups of coffee and tea, respectively. They peer at the office tenant marquee, scanning it for Madilyn's office.

A deep baritone voice speaks over their shoulders. "You folks need any help?" The voice startles them. He's a Security Guard.

"No. No we're fine, sir. Just confirming our meeting location," says Dr. Du Bois. Dr. Fulani smiles, a bit relieved that he isn't a threat.

"Your voice is so deep. Scared me."

"I hear that all the time. Heard I should do radio." He returns a smile as he walks off.

Dr. Du Bois watches the guard walk away, then quickly turns to Dr. Fulani. "She's on the fifth floor." Dr. Du Bois looks at his watch. It reads 11:55AM. "We don't have much time."

The elevator dings as the floor indicator marquee illuminates, signaling "5". The doors open, then Dr. Du Bois and Dr. Fulani slowly exit the elevator into the fifth-floor corridor. They look down the corridor and spot the US FDA office. The office suite has a glass door.

Through the glass, they see the East Indian Man from the café. He sits in the waiting area and casually flips through a magazine.

"I have a plan. Not really, but just follow my lead," says Dr. Du Bois. He looks at his watch. It reads 12:00PM. They walk with a brisk pace toward the suite as the Receptionist gets up from his desk.

Perfectly timed, they reach the suite door and listen for his name. "Mr. Patel. Madilyn will see you now," says the Receptionist. Dr. Du Bois throws his hands in the air, whispering to Dr. Fulani. "Awesome. There has to be millions of Patels."

"Got another idea," replies Dr. Fulani. He looks puzzled as she walks off. Dr. Fulani sneaks into the reception area as the Receptionist escorts Mr. Patel down the hallway. Dr. Du Bois stands inside at the door.

She peeks at the guest sign-in sheet. It reads "Vijay Patel". Dr. Fulani turns to leave. Dr. Du Bois opens the door for Dr. Fulani. As they exit, the Receptionist returns to the reception area. "Hey. Can I help you guys?"

Dr. Fulani improvises, "Yes. We're looking for CBRE?" Dr. Fulani throws her hands up. She appears confused and frustrated. "I thought they were on the fifth floor?"

The Receptionist smiles, "No. They're one level down on the fourth floor." Dr. Fulani smiles. "Thanks!"

The elevator quietly glides down to the lobby as the floors countdown on the marquee. Dr. Du Bois and Dr. Fulani are alone on the elevator. They are silent for a moment.

"Well played, ma'am."

"You too, sir."

They fist bump.

Late in the evening, back at their hotel, Dr. Du Bois and Dr. Fulani sit on separate beds. They eat room service ordered meals.

"I wonder what our Ukrainian friend is up to," Dr. Du Bois asks.

"Please, don't speak him up."

Dr. Du Bois finishes his meal. He takes a seat at the desk, then opens their laptop. Dr. Fulani looks at him as she bites into a lettuce wrap.

"What are you about to do?"

"Find out what Google says about Vijay." Dr. Fulani watches him from the bed as she eats her vegan meal.

Dr. Du Bois types "Vijay Patel" into the Google search box. He filters the search to "images", then scrolls through to find a photo of Vijay. He finds one, then clicks the link to an article.

"Wow."

"What is it?"

Dr. Fulani sits her meal aside. She grabs a chair and sits next to Dr. Du Bois. They gaze at the laptop screen.

Vijay Patel
CEO of Uni-Ceutical Laboratories
Headquartered in Atlanta, GA

He looks at Dr. Fulani. "Ever heard of them?" Dr. Fulani shakes her head, negatively, then shrugs. Dr. Du Bois sits back in his chair brooding for a moment. "They're in Atlanta."

Dr. Du Bois strolls over to the window. There is a beautiful panoramic view of a moonlit Lake Michigan. He stares out of the window pensively. Hands clasped behind his back like a dignitary.

"We need to find more evidence."

"Take some pictures of them together to start."

"Yes. Exactly."

Dr. Fulani walks over to the window with him. She sips her tea and gazes out of the window.

"Such a beautiful city."

"It is."

"As a little girl growing up in small-town Tennessee, I dreamed about living somewhere like Chicago. All the lights, massive buildings."

"Founded by Jean-Baptiste Point DuSable."

Dr. Fulani looks at Dr. Du Bois. "You're like a walking encyclopedia. You know that, Geoffrey?"

"Interesting. I was once called a Negropedia."

She laughs.

He smiles. "My ex-wife didn't like that. She called me a self-absorbed know-it-all."

Dr. Du Bois shrugs it off, then continues, "Pretty strong words for a man that just enjoys to read books."

"I think it's attractive actually."

Dr. Du Bois looks at her, but remains silent.

"No. I mean, it's cool that you're smart. Nothing to be ashamed of," she adds.

Dr. Du Bois nods affirmatively.

"These days women like intelligent men. We like someone that can match our intellect."

"Indeed, geek is in, now. Worked to my advantage in a few situations, if I recall correctly."

Dr. Fulani smiles. They continue to gaze out of the window at the Chicago skyline and Lake Michigan.

"Did I ever tell you why I pursued holistic practices instead of traditional medicine?"

"No."

"You first."

Dr. Fulani looks at him. "The ancestors." She shrugs. He looks at her curiously to expound.

She continues, "It's what our ancestors practiced."

"Indeed. Prior to modern medicine, yes." He nods affirmatively. "It always amazes me how people forget that," he continues.

"Or just ignorant to it."

"What was your spark?"

"A trip to Africa."

"Wow."

"When I was a senior in high school, we took a trip to Nigeria."

"Interesting."

"It's the reason I dropped the slave name."

Dr. Du Bois laughs. "What was your name before?"

She looks blankly at Dr. Du Bois. "Trisha Compton." They both laugh.

The laughter fades. Dr. Du Bois silences for a moment. "So, my mother, a hardworking English teacher for 30 years." He smiles uncomfortably, then continues, "She was a grammar and speech Nazi! Speak in complete sentences; no slang; pronounce your words! Or you had to write a book report." He laughs. Dr. Fulani listens and smiles warmly.

In a more somber tone, he continues, "She was diagnosed with cancer. The chemo provided no progress. None!"

"I'm sorry, Geoffrey."

"I was reading a book at the time called the Sunfood Way to Health." Dr. Du Bois holds his head low.

"I took my first steps toward veganism after reading that," says Dr. Fulani.

"Yeah. Before reading that, I didn't believe in holistic health. My mother referred to it as witchcraft!"

They both laugh. "Seriously, she once called me a witch doctor!" They continue to laugh.

He quiets for a moment, then returns to a more serious tone. "I started her on a raw diet, mostly green vegetables, juices, supplements, black seed oil, detoxing; provided her with moderate exercise and a few hours of relaxation in the sun during the day. She started to drastically improve!"

Dr. Du Bois stares out of the window with glazed eyes. "But it was too late." Dr. Fulani rubs

Dr. Du Bois' shoulder. "The cancer had advanced too far."

He looks at Dr. Fulani. "Have I depressed you enough?

"No. That was compelling, Geoffrey."

Dr. Du Bois smiles teary eyed. He hugs Dr. Fulani very tight. They look at each other passionately for a moment, studying each other's eyes. They kiss.

A sunny but cool morning at Millennium Park, Dr. Du Bois and Dr. Fulani sit on a park bench across from Madilyn's office. Still discreet in appearance, they stare at the building directly across the street, sipping coffee and tea. The steam from their cups is more pronounced in the colder air.

Dr. Du Bois' cell phone pings with a text message. He reaches in his pocket, appearing a bit surprised. He looks at the phone.

"No! Hell no!"

"What is it?"

Dr. Du Bois hands her the cellphone shaking his head in disbelief. Dr. Fulani looks at the phone. The sender reads "Justin Jakehorne". The message simply reads, "hey".

"What!?" Dr. Fulani yells. They both nervously peer around. Their hearts race and beat rapidly in unison.

"Impossible. We saw his body," Dr. Fulani continues.

"Let me think a bit."

"And why do you still have your cellphone, Geoffrey?"

Dr. Fulani pulls out a small phone. Dr. Du Bois looks at her phone; looks at his phone; then looks at her. Still shocked from the ominous message. He's speechless.

"You should have a prepaid," lectures Dr. Fulani.

Amidst the exchange, Madilyn walks out of the building. Dr. Du Bois spots her.

"Look! Look! There she is!" So excited and anxious, he spills his coffee. "Dammit!" As he attempts to wipe the coffee off Vijay Patel follows Madilyn out of the front entrance. Dr. Fulani brings it to his attention, "Vijay too!"

Coffee all over his pants, Dr. Du Bois chucks the cup in Millennium Park. He looks at his cellphone, then tucks it into his pocket.

Madilyn and Vijay casually stroll down Michigan Avenue. Dr. Du Bois and Dr. Fulani lurk from the opposite side of the street as they follow them.

"They're talking," whispers Dr. Fulani.

"Yeah, we need to hear that conversation."

Dr. Fulani snaps a few pictures of them with her camera. The distance between them widens as Madilyn and Vijay pick up their pace. Dr. Du Bois and Dr. Fulani walk faster.

Madilyn and Vijay walk over the DuSable Bridge crossing the Chicago River. Dr. Du Bois and Dr. Fulani get closer to them. Another text message pings Dr. Du Bois' phone. He looks down at the cellphone as they cross the bridge. The message from Justin Jakehorne reads "where r u guys?"

Dr. Fulani looks at the message.

"Should we respond? Give a false location?"

"No. It's a trap. I think he's lost our trail. We know for certain Justin is dead."

Dr. Du Bois looks around. He looks up in the sky, then at a cellphone tower.

"If we respond, the signal will bounce off the nearest cell tower and he'll be able to triangulate our location."

"Right! I think I saw that in a movie."

Dr. Du Bois looks down at the green tinted Chicago River passing under the bridge. He looks at Dr. Fulani, then tosses his phone over the bridge. He watches as it splashes into the water.

Madilyn and Vijay reach a corner. The light turns red before they arrive so they stop and chat for a bit. Dr. Du Bois and Dr. Fulani stand a few feet away. They sneak closer through the small crowd. Dr. Fulani begins to record their conversation with her prepaid smartphone.

"When should I expect that next payment?" probes Madilyn.

"In a few days."

"You said that last week!! Stop bullshitting me, Vijay! I approved—." Madilyn looks over her shoulders. She continues in a lower voice, "—I approved that Dynotriol shit with no clinical trials."

"I know, Madilyn. I know."

"None. Not one! And I need that money!"

"I know."

"It could be fucking killing people for all I know." Madilyn lights a cigarette.

Vijay looks around, then whispers, "It's not. I'm sure of that. Take it myself." Vijay pulls out a metal pill vial. He shakes the bottle rattling the pills, giving a smug shrug.

"That's the third one this month, Vijay."

"And I'm not bullshitting you by the way."

They cross the street. Dr. Du Bois and Dr. Fulani follow behind. She continues to record.

"There's a certain procedure we follow for payment on these transactions." Vijay responds.

"What about the Russian? Heard any updates yet?"

Vijay looks over his shoulder cautiously. By chance, he makes direct eye contact with Dr. Fulani when he turns around.

Dr. Fulani smiles and holds the phone high pretending to take a selfie. She fluffs her afro. Dr. Du Bois gives a fake cough and looks away. Vijay turns back around and continues the conversation.

Dr. Fulani and Dr. Du Bois breathe a sigh of relief. They drop back a few paces. They record one last segment.

"He has a few more to go. What do you think we should do when it's all done though?" Vijay asks.

"Good question. He knows more about Operation Hygieia than he should."

Vijay shrugs. "We can always hire another?"

"You're cold." Madilyn laughs. "I love that though."

"Was just thinking, how would Madilyn handle it?" They both laugh. Madilyn and Vijay walk past a building with reflective windows.

Vijay looks at his reflection in the window as they walk past the building to check himself out. His confirms that his tailored suit fits well. He catches glimpse of Dr. Fulani and Dr. Du Bois several feet behind. Vijay leans in and whispers to Madilyn.

"I think we're being followed." He places his hand on her shoulder. "Don't turn around though." Madilyn nods. "OK. Let's change the subject."

Vijay turns around. Dr. Fulani and Dr. Du Bois are no longer behind them.

An open bottle of champagne sits in an ice bucket on a table at a hotel room. Two champagne glasses sit adjacent. Dr. Du Bois and Dr. Fulani sit at the desk. Her phone is connected to the laptop.

"Let's get that video saved," says Dr. Du Bois.

"Before Justin texts my phone."

Dr. Du Bois points at her. "Being texted from a dead man's phone. That was ominous. Sent chills down my spine."

"So, she mentioned Dynotriol again. What else do you know about it?" Dr. Fulani asks. Dr. Du Bois shrugs. She types "Dynotriol" in the Google search box. "Let's see…"

Dynotriol: A stimulant known for its cognitive enhancing abilities.

Dr. Fulani clicks another article on the gross sales netted from the medication. They read the screen.

"Since its recent launch, Dynotriol sales have been phenomenal, netting about $5.7 million. As a result, stock prices have been skyrocketing…"

"Oh my God!" Dr. Fulani drops her head.

"What's the matter?"

"Those numbers." She pulls a book from her purse, then throws it on the table.

"Those numbers are why they want me..." She shakes her head.

Dr. Du Bois looks at the cover. It reads "1001 Nootropic Alternatives to Smart Drugs by Dr. Ola Fulani."

"I've researched natural nootropic alternatives that can provide long term cognitive benefits," she adds.

"Interesting."

"Now we know why we're both blacklisted!"

Dr. Du Bois looks at Dr. Fulani.

"Did you catch that reference from Madilyn? Operation..."

"Operation Hygieia."

"Hygieia? Interesting."

"Very interesting name for this operation."

"You're right. She's the Greek goddess of health, cleanliness, and hy—."

"They view these fucking murders as 'cleaning' up?" yells Dr. Fulani.

"Insane."

"I mean. How could they do this? We help people? We're fucking doctors too?" Dr. Fulani slams her champagne glass down and continues.

"Makes me wonder if they killed Dr. Sebi too!"

"That's right! Hadn't thought about that. Wow."

Dr. Du Bois shows a mixed emotion of anger and sadness. "I mean, no moral compass whatsoever. No ethic. Just callous."

"Right!"

"If I were a religious man, I would say they'd burn for this."

"Do you believe in Karma?"

Dr. Du Bois sips his champagne. "I don't 'believe' it. It's science!" Raising a finger to drive his point home.

"Well, there you have it. They will pay then."

Dr. Du Bois nods, then points angrily. "I'll make goddamn sure of it!" Dr. Fulani appears surprised by the intensity. She smiles. A news story plays on the television which gets their attention.

"We have some breaking news," says the CNN News Anchor. They both look at the television. "Turn that up." Dr. Du Bois grabs the remote and turns it up.

"Another alternative medicine doctor has gone missing. Dr. Ola Fulani from right here in Atlanta, Georgia."

Dr. Du Bois yells, "What?!"

The CNN News Anchor continues, "We will provide more details as they develop."

"I guess they don't care about me." Dr. Du Bois quips. Dr. Fulani smiles, but not sure how to react to the news.

"Your daughter? Your family? They know you're OK?" Dr. Du Bois asks.

"Yeah. They know I'm safe. I'll reach out to my daughter though so she knows for certain after this news story."

"Good."

Dr. Du Bois tops off their champagne glasses. He takes one for himself and hands the other to Dr. Fulani. They raise their glasses.

"What are we celebrating, exactly?" Dr. Fulani's now thoroughly confused.

"To another day above ground, and another day of progress."

"OK." Dr. Fulani nods.

"Ola, I've never felt more fortunate to be alive. Cherishing each day as I always should have."

He takes off his bowtie and unbuttons his shirt collar. Dr. Du Bois has lived a sheltered life, purposefully closing himself off from the world, absorbed with his passion for wellness, but the threat of death now has him treasuring each moment of life like never before.

Dr. Fulani nods, appearing to relish his new outlook. She offers a toast. "Afya!"

He appears puzzled, then reluctantly returns the toast, "Afya?"

She giggles. "That's a toast in Swahili. A toast to good health and wellness!"

Dr. Du Bois nods affirmatively. "Fitting!" He rubs his beard. He raises his glass high. "Yes. To that!" They both laugh.

Madilyn stands near her office window, gazing at the nighttime view of Millennium Park and Lake Michigan. The office walls are covered with degrees, plaques, and certificates of accomplishment. She holds a glass of whiskey staring at an airplane traversing the sky.

She sips and intensely watches it trek south, almost as if she's imagining being on that plane. Her cellphone rings on her desk interrupting her daydream. She takes a sip as she walks back to her desk.

With no intention of answering, she casually peeks at it. The name reads "Sharon Mathers." Madilyn's eyes bulge. She sits down, takes a deep breath. She takes another deep breath, then answers.

"Sharon," says Madilyn warmly.

"Yes. It's me." Sharon replies in a raspy voice. The sound of someone who's been crying interminably.

"How you holding up, girl?"

"I'm holding. That's all I can say."

"They're gonna find this psychopath responsible. You just hang in there."

"That's why I'm calling actually."

Madilyn sits up nervously. "About the psychopath?"

"I wish. No, I'm calling to tell you about Simon's funeral arrangements."

"Oh. OK, of course."

"I'll just text them to you actually."

"OK. That works. You hang in there, Sharon."

"Thanks Madilyn!"

"Call me if you need me."

"Will do."

Madilyn hangs up the phone, then tosses it on the desk. It lands on a medical bill on the corner of her desk. She picks it up and stares at it. It shows a past due balance of $55,113. She tosses it aside and shakes her head.

She takes a sip of whiskey, then slides open a desk drawer. A 38-caliber revolver lies in the drawer next to a black nondescript cellphone. Madilyn stares in the drawer for several moments.

She reaches into the drawer and pulls out the cellphone. She places a call. "I need you to step things up on Hygieia. I think someone is following me." She hangs up immediately, throws the phone in the drawer, then slams it shut.

Madilyn thinks about Sharon momentarily. Sharon works in the US FDA office in Atlanta. They met at a conference about a year ago, and they've since kept in touch sporadically. Madilyn didn't know Sharon was married to Simon, until the media released his family details after his death. Madilyn muses as she twirls her glass of whiskey.

8

EMBERS OF EBERS PAPYRUS

A black Rolls-Royce Dawn Drophead Coupé cruises down Peachtree Street in downtown Atlanta. It's late in the afternoon. Country Boy drives while Skrill rides shotgun. He's about 6'-3" at 300-lbs so he fills the front seat completely. He wears a black t-shirt, draped with a diamond encrusted chain. It's embellished with a large stylized "B" as the charm. Fitting since he is referred to as "B" by his close friends. He grew up with Skrill on the south side of Atlanta. Now a world renown Rapper, he continues to keep his friends close.

"That's fucked up about your cousin man, damn!" Skrill consoles.

"Yeah." He fist bumps Skrill. "Preciate you."

"How old was he?"

"Young! Man, only nineteen. And he was a fucking GENIUS!"

"Damn."

"And that shit ain't true they saying on the news!"

"Right, niggas don't do that kinda shit."

"Yeah, somebody did that. If I get a line on 'em, I'm gone let you know."

Skrill nods in approval as he hits a blunt. "Where your next spot on the tour?" He exhales, then passes it.

"The Chi, then Detroit."

Skrill looks around at the elegant interior of the Rolls-Royce. "You done made it my nigga!"

"Preciate you folk. Never got so many damn checks in my life!" He raps a tune, "Checks, checks, checks, checks." They both laugh. Country Boy pulls into the parking lot of a café. He backs into a parking space.

"Bout to pick up one now, actually."

"Check?"

"Yup. Gimme about fifteen. Bout to run up in here holla at this nigga real quick."

"OK folk."

As Country Boy heads inside the café for his meeting, Skrill sinks back into the seat relaxing.

The table that Country Boy and his guest takes inside the café is visible in the passenger side mirror. Skrill doesn't see them initially, but catches glimpse as they are seated.

He watches them in the mirror. He can't quite see who he's meeting with so he turns around to get a better look. He sees Country Boy sitting at a table across from an East Indian fellow in a tailored suit. He thinks nothing of it, then turns back around.

45 Minutes Later…

Country Boy gets back in the car. Skrill looks at the time on his cell phone, then shakes his head. He puns Country Boy on a separate matter.

"So…you getting checks from the Taliban my nigga?" They both laugh.

"Nah, I think he a Indian…like from India and shit," replies Country Boy. He reaches for the blunt.

"That's your A&R?"

"Nah, he run a pharmaceutical company." Country Boy tokes and coughs.

Skrill, still perplexed, looks puzzled as he tries to figure it out. He gives up.

"Fuck he paying you for then??"

Country Boy takes another slow pull on the blunt. "Shit…promoting pills on my records."

Skrill goes silent and blank, digesting what he's just heard. He thinks about his son being caught with prescription drugs. He ponders Country Boy's recent hit songs that readily drop various brands of prescription drugs for recreational use.

"Gave me some new shit too. Supposed to be like Molly," continues Country Boy. He produces a pill bottle. Skrill just glares at it.

Country Boy continues, "…AND he gave me some shit, supposed to make your memory better. Dyno…dyno something. I'm a call these mufuckas DINOSAURS!" He lets off a hearty laugh. Skrill just gives a faint smirk.

"Want this?" Country Boy hands a pill bottle to him, labeled Dynotriol.

Skrill fans his hand away. "Nah, I'm good folk."

Country Boy turns to look at him directly. "Fuck wrong with you, nigga?" Country Boy appears disappointed.

"I'm good with the blunts, B. Don't want no pills." Skrill turns and looks at him directly. "That's some ole white girl shit anyway. Popping fucking pills."

Country Boy silences for a brief moment, then looks back at Skrill. "Boy, if you don't stop acting like one of these OLD Negroes." They both laugh.

They cruise to a red light. Skrill continues to peer out of the window smoking his blunt. He's processing all that's just transpired. In the background, Country Boy works on a hook for his latest drug. *"Popping purple dinosaurs, fucking hoes on the floor…"* As they sit at the light, Skrill looks at the car idling next to them. The driver casually waves at him. Skrill just nods in acknowledgment. Country Boy speeds off.

The driver in the car next to them watches their car speed off. The driver is Viktor.

The Hartsfield-Jackson International Airport bustles with travelers just after dusk. Dr. Du Bois and Dr. Fulani exit the airport terminal pulling their roller bags. "Feels much better here," says Dr. Du Bois.

The mysterious guy from their flight to Chicago lurks in a corner smoking a cigarillo. He watches them as he chats on a cellphone. Dr. Fulani and Dr. Du Bois do not see him.

"How long before our Lyft arrives?" Dr. Du Bois asks.

Dr. Fulani looks at the app on her phone. "Just a few minutes." Dr. Du Bois walks to the curb and looks down the lane for their ride.

"Hey. That's it pulling up now." She pulls her roller bag to the curb. "The silver Toyota." The car pulls up to the curb and pops the trunk. The doctors load their bags inside, then hop in the back seat. The Lyft vehicle drives off from the terminal.

"Right on time. You're getting a huge tip for this," exclaims Dr. Du Bois. The Lyft driver is silent for a moment as he enters the highway. A pair of steely blue eyes glower at Dr. Du Bois in the rearview mirror.

"I have already the biggest tip of the night," exults the Lyft driver. He speaks with a pronounced Ukrainian accent.

Paralyzed by shock, Dr. Fulani and Dr. Du Bois freeze, staring at the back of the head of the mysterious Lyft driver. He adjusts the rearview mirror for them to see his face. It's Viktor. He gives them a cold stare. The Ukrainian tattoo visible on his throat.

He produces a gun, then turns to point it at them casually.

"You make this harder than it should be for me." He turns back to continue driving.

"You don't have to do this, Mr. Kalashnik," pleads Dr. Du Bois.

"You even know my last name? You're a smart little man. Or not so smart." Viktor sucks his teeth.

Viktor turns back around and aggressively points the gun at Dr. Du Bois. He yells demands. "Give me your laptops and information from your trip!" Dr. Du Bois hesitates. Viktor casually fires a silenced round into the seat between Dr. Fulani and Dr. Du Bois. They both jump and scream. "OK! OK!" Dr. Du Bois frantically stutters. He scrambles to pull their laptop out of the bag.

"No! Give me whole bag!" Viktor demands. He directs with his gun. "Sit in front seat." Dr. Du Bois obliges and sits his laptop bag in the front seat. Dr. Fulani sheds a few tears.

Viktor looks at Dr. Du Bois in the rearview mirror as he turns his attention back to the road. "You are much harder to kill than your cousin, Skill. Wrong name for him. He has no skill."

Dr. Du Bois glares at Viktor. His fear transforms to anger. "What did you just say?" Dr. Fulani looks at Dr. Du Bois. She places her hand on his leg. Viktor continues his taunting. "Your cousin. I came to his house looking for you." Viktor narrates the flashback scene.

"I didn't find you, but your cousin got in my way..."

Skrill sat on his couch with a young thug with locks and a brawny female thug. He rolled a blunt.

A silenced bullet fired through the window. The young thug fell over on the table. He was shot in the head. Blood soaked his locks.

"I crushed his gangsters like cockroaches..."

The brawny female thug jumped up from the couch and pulled her gun from her waistband.

A silenced bullet fired through the window. She slumped to the floor from a headshot.

"Crushed them one by one..."
Skrill dove on the floor. He reached under the coffee table and pulled out a fully-automatic assault rifle.

Kneeled on a single knee at the base of his couch, Skrill fired rounds violently through the window defending his home. Brass 5.56-caliber shells carpeted the living room floor as they bounced and clanked all over. Skrill paused his wild assault and took cover behind the couch.

A blanket of silence covered the living room. His ears rang from the resounding boom of his weapon. Skrill peeked out of the windowless pane.

"I creep..."
Viktor walked up behind Skrill. He placed the barrel of his gun on the back of his head. Skrill felt the barrel tight on his skull. With a defiant screw-face, Skrill berated him, "Fuck you! Russian, potato vodka drinking mother—!"

Viktor fired a single silenced shot before he could finish.

Dr. Du Bois and Dr. Fulani listen in disbelief. Viktor looks at Dr. Du Bois directly in the eyes through the rearview mirror. "Your cousin. He scream like little girl when I killed him." Dr. Du Bois seethes with anger.

Viktor continues his morbid story. "Like little black cockroaches. They are still on bottom of my shoe."

Dr. Du Bois lunges at Viktor grabbing the gun. They wrestle for control of the weapon.

A round fires, shattering the front passenger window. Dr. Fulani screams. The car swerves on the highway. They continue to wrestle for control of the pistol.

The car veers onto the shoulder. Suddenly, it crashes into the end of a metal guardrail. The gun falls to the front floor. Viktor and Dr. Du Bois are temporarily stunned and disoriented.

Dr. Fulani was wearing her seatbelt so she's fine. She kicks open the back door. "Geoffrey! Let's go." She grabs his arm as she flees from the car. Viktor reaches for the gun. Dr. Fulani and Dr. Du Bois bolt from the vehicle leaving everything behind.

Viktor squeezes off a random silenced shot as they run. It zips past Dr. Du Bois' ear. He screams. They dart into a wooded area off of the highway. Two silenced bullets zip past them hitting tree branches.

Dr. Fulani runs much faster than Dr. Du Bois. He trails her by a few feet. She sprints with the poise of Florence Griffith Joyner. She clears a log in their path like a hurdle. Dr. Du Bois barely clears it. "Come on, Geoffrey!"

She reaches the Chattahoochee River. Dr. Du Bois arrives a few moments later. Dr. Fulani looks at the span to the other side.

"Son-of-a-bitch!"

It's about 200 feet and the current flows rapidly. Dr. Du Bois, breathing heavily, struggles to get his words out. "This is a low point. We can walk across. I kayak through here sometimes."

Dr. Du Bois holds Dr. Fulani's hand guiding her across. She holds up her dress from the water with her other hand. They wade across the river and continue into a deeply wooded area. The doctors rest for a moment against a tree, keeping watch on the river for Viktor. Dr. Du Bois still breathing heavily, inquires.

"So, you've run track I take it?"

"Yeah, but I wasn't gonna leave you. Don't worry."

"We should continue on."

They stand up and brush off the debris. Suddenly a branch cracks on the ground in the distance.

"Oh God! What was that?" whispers Dr. Fulani.

"Don't worry. We'll be fine."

They hold hands as they slowly trek through the woods. Grass rustles as something sprints towards them. Dr. Du Bois shields Dr. Fulani.

It's a deer. It scurries past them. "Let's get the hell out of here."

Outside an apartment complex on the south side of Atlanta, several police cars and a Crime Scene Investigation van are parked in the parking lot. Detective Mercer approaches the apartment. Yellow crime scene tape surrounds the yard.

Officer Carlyle stands outside the entrance to the apartment. He wears a lustrous Bvlgari watch. As Detective Mercer approaches him, he quips. "Look like a card game got out of hand. Case closed?"

Detective Mercer doesn't return a smile as he walks past him. He looks at the shiny new watch on Officer Carlyle's wrist, then looks at Officer Carlyle.

Blood spatter covers the living room walls and floors. Brass 5.56-caliber shells litter the room. The dead bodies of two Black males and a female lay sprawled about the living room. The Older Detective is present taking notes, smoking a pipe.

Detective Mercer looks at him. "What we got?" He kneels down looking at the body of one of the

Black males. He chews his gum fervently as he continues, "Head shot here apparently. Close range." Detective Mercer peers around the room taking in the scene.

The Older Detective points at the living room window with his pipe. "Trajectory of the bullets came from this window here." Detective Mercer nods affirmatively. The Older Detective continues, "But get this. Three shots. Three kills. No other incoming shots."

Detective Mercer stops chewing. He appears as though he's seen a ghost. He looks at the Older Detective.

"Any shell casings found outside?"

"Damn good point. Nope. Not a one."

Detective Mercer stands up, "Whose place is this?" As he looks around the room.

The Older Detective flips through his notes. "Looks like it belongs to ummm...ummm er uhh." Detective Mercer is getting impatient.

He continues, "...umm Todd...ummm...Du Bois." Butchering the pronunciation as he points with his pipe. "That fella with his head blown wide open. Actually, I picked him up just the other day."

Detective Mercer stares at the Older Detective.

9

TWILIGHT OF THE GODS

Silverware clanks plates during a busy brunch hour at the Old Lady Gang restaurant. The southern-styled eatery is nestled in the trendy Castleberry Hill neighborhood of Atlanta. Dr. Du Bois and Dr. Fulani are amongst the brunch hour patrons. They eat breakfast and sip their coffee and green tea, respectively. She has oatmeal and toast which she consumes gracefully. He has southern-styled fried chicken, which he tears into unapologetically. He's a nervous eater.

Partially concealing their identities, Dr. Fulani wears a scarf on her head with sunglasses. Dr. Du Bois wears a driver's hat snugly on his head.

Paranoid, they continuously glance over their shoulders.

"Can't believe we lost ALL of our evidence." Dr. Fulani shakes her head as she eats a spoonful of oatmeal.

"We didn't lose our lives though," adds Dr. Du Bois, with a greasy finger raised driving home his point. Dr. Fulani doesn't look impressed with his response.

She looks at his plate. "I thought you were a pescatarian."

"90% of the time, yes. The other 10% I'm pollo-pescatarian." He takes a few more bites, then ponders a bit.

"You'd think with his distinctive throat tatt the cops could search some sort of database, though right?" Dr. Du Bois continues as he shakes his head.

"Maybe he has no criminal record in the States." Dr. Fulani shrugs.

"Good point."

"Or maybe he has someone with the authority to expunge it."

"Another good point!"

The bell dings on the door as a customer enters. They both jump and nervously turn to look. Dr. Du Bois wipes his hands, then pulls out a flash drive and sits it on the table.

"Seriously?" She drops the spoon in her bowl.

Dr. Du Bois dispiritedly shakes his head. "Unfortunately, I don't think it'll be of much use."

"Why not?"

"It was tucked in my shoe during the running and wading through water."

"Fuck!" She sits back in her seat.

"The information we have. It's up here." Dr. Du Bois points at his head.

Dr. Fulani side-eyes him. "That won't hold up in court, Geoffrey."

"We have just enough information to get representation and counsel at the very least," retorts Dr. Du Bois.

The bell on the door dings as another customer enters. They both jump and nervously turn to look. They munch on their breakfast for a few bites.

"You know, I started some new research...before all of this went down," Dr. Fulani says.

"What's it about?" Dr. Du Bois asks as he mangles the chicken on his plate.

"The psychological effects of systemic racism and white supremacy, and how they in turn affect our physical and mental health." She sips her tea.

Dr. Du Bois slows his chewing. "Bit of a stretch, don't you think?"

"No, why?"

"I mean..."

"Geoffrey."

Dr. Du Bois shakes his head and focuses on eating his chicken. Dr. Fulani stares at him realizing how ingenuous and guileless he can be at times when it comes to progressive theories regarding race; however, this entire ordeal is making him evolve a bit and he's more inclined to believe ideas that are inconceivable to him on the surface.

"Cortisol?" Dr. Fulani continues.

"Yes."

"Is it not one of the main hormones released by the adrenal gland in response to stress?"

"Ah yes!"

"And isn't racism and the systemic conditions it create, HELLA stressful for Black folks?"

"Indeed yes." He raises a greasy finger "I see where you're going. Great theory, Ola."

"Is EVERYTHING about science with you, Geoffrey?" She laughs.

"It is actually."

The bell on the door dings as another customer enters. They both jump and nervously turn to look.

A white Airbus Helicopters H135 with the Uni-Ceutical Laboratory's logo brandished on the side, chops the sky. It glides over the City of

Atlanta on a clear day. The luxurious interior features white leather seats and wood grain accents.

Vijay sits with his arm around his girlfriend, Amirah. She's in her late twenties and also East Indian. He's dressed in tailored slacks with a collared shirt and sleeves rolled; she's draped in a purple silk traditional saree. They stare out of the window. Vijay doesn't appear relaxed. He appears to have something heavy on his mind.

"Such a beautiful view of Atlanta! Oh my gosh!" exclaims Amirah. Vijay looks at her as she enjoys the view; he's silent. There's an awkward silence, so Amirah looks at him.

"Why are you so quiet?"

Vijay looks at her, then looks around the chopper. "Am I good enough for your father now?" He raises his hand gloating about his luxury helicopter.

"What?"

"Good enough to marry you?"

"Stop it, Vijay. It's not about that."

"Oh? What's it about then?"

"That's not what I mean."

"It's because I was born 'untouchable.' I know."

"What are you talking about?"

"That's why I've worked so hard."

"He's just a stubborn jerk, Vijay. It's not that deep."

"He's not that simple either."
"You're overthinking this."
Vijay pours a glass of wine from the decanter.
tares out of the window thinking about the
n at hand. Amirah comes from a royal
and Vijay knows this. Vijay has done
vell for himself financially, albeit some
Her family's net worth is nearly ten
iiay's and he knows this as well.
has a history of "strategically
marriages with coequally
didn't pass the vetting
ugh this has not been
him, he senses this to

e
il.
he

with

p. She
s a bite,
BELIEVE

next to a small
cts off the
andeliers,

eping
ion
e

headquarters
with a design
here is also a
ling three-story
sen by the CEO,
sion for aviation.
ht white-on-white
ings from a lanyard

Chuck on his head, then proceeds up the staircase.

Madilyn walks down the hallway. She butts open a door, gently. "Honey, you still awake?" Madilyn enters Maggie's bedroom. The room is decorated to fancy a young adolescent girl. The unfortunate focal point of the room is the medical equipment surrounding a large pink bed.

Underneath the equipment in the center of th bed, lies nine-year-old Maggie, bald and fra Maggie smiles when she sees Madilyn and tiramisu cake.

"I brought you your favorite."

"Thank you, mommy!" Maggie claps excitement.

Madilyn smiles and helps Maggie sit feeds her the milk and cake. Madilyn tak then feeds one to Maggie. "You won't the day I've had…"

Uni-Ceutical Laboratory's consists of a large white building resembling an aircraft hangar. helipad on the roof of the spra structure. The design was cho Vijay Patel, because of his pas

A guy walks down the br corridor. His name badge s

around his neck as he walks. "Uni-Ceutical Laboratory" is sprawled along the corridor wall with metal letters. The guy shakes his head at the redundancy, as he approaches the reception desk. The badge swinging from his neck reads, "John Hanson, Macon Times Newspaper."

The guy is revealed to be Dr. Du Bois, concealing his identity with a pair of partially tinted glasses, cap, and a Macon Times t-shirt. He rehearses a southern accent in his head briefly. The receptionist stands as he reaches the desk.

"Good afternoon."

"Good afternoon, sir. I'm here to see Mr. Westmoreland."

"OK. He'll be right with you. Just sign in here."

"Thank you, sir."

Dr. Du Bois signs-in, then sits on a sofa. He mindlessly flips through a pharmaceutical magazine. Not even focusing on the pages, he thinks about his once normal life.

A few moments later, the receptionist stands up, interrupting his daydream.

"Mr. Hanson."

"Yessir?"

"He's ready to see you. Follow me."

The lead scientist at the lab, Egbert Westmoreland, Caucasian-American man in his fifties, sits at his desk. He's dressed in a lab coat and looks sternly at Dr. Du Bois. He's pale and roughly shaven appearing to spend most of his life in the lab. Dr. Du Bois sits across from him holding a clipboard.

"I promise not to take too much of your time, sir. Just want to bring a good story back home to good ole Macon."

Egbert lightens up a bit. "I could use a break from that damn lab. And I'm from Macon actually, so I couldn't refuse."

"Yeah?" Dr. Du Bois appears nervous. "Love it down there."

"Miss it sometimes."

"Not much has changed."

"So, what's your favorite place to grub?"

Dr. Du Bois hesitates for a moment. "Uh, so many to choose from…" Dr. Du Bois nervously shuffles his papers. Egbert looks at him for a response.

"I got to go with…um…Me-Maws."

Egbert snaps his finger, then points at Dr. Du Bois. "Me-Maws' the SHIT! Let's get started."

His choice of words catches Dr. Du Bois off guard, supplanting his prior anxiety. "OK…" He looks down at his clipboard.

"OK, so, tell me a little about Uni-Ceutical Labs."

"Let's see. We formed in 2007. Our mission is unifying pharmaceutical companies under one umbrella."

"I see." Dr. Du Bois rubs his beard. "And how do ya'll accomplish this?"

"Primarily through acquisitions of smaller companies." Egbert nods proudly.

"So, you guys are like, a pharmaceutical conglomerate?"

"Something like that, yeah, but we ain't breaking any Anti-Trust laws."

"Dynotriol." Dr. Du Bois observes Egbert closely when he mentions the drug. Egbert appears very relaxed. "What about it?"

"I read on the web that you netted close to six million dollars in sales?"

Egbert laughs. "We've actually seen a spike recently." Dr. Du Bois nervously drops his clipboard. "Sorry. What do you mean?"

"Within the last year, to date, we've seen a jump up to about twelve mil."

Dr. Du Bois' face tenses. He shifts uncomfortably.

Egbert continues. "I'm not really a numbers guy though. Vijay Patel, our CEO; he could tell you all about our numbers." Egbert looks at the time on his cell phone. "Actually, he's available now. His next meeting is a half-hour from now." Egbert picks up the receiver on his office phone to dial Vijay's extension.

"No, no, no. Don't want to bother the big ole 'CEO' just for a Macon Times news story." Dr. Du Bois laughs nervously. He looks at his watch. He isn't wearing one.

"Got another interview soon. I think that's just about all I need right now," says Dr. Du Bois as he stands up. He extends his hand to Egbert.

"Thank you for your time, sir." They shake.

"Not a problem. Anytime." Egbert rubs his belly. "You got me wanting some Me-Maw's now." Dr. Du Bois smiles.

As Dr. Du Bois walks past the reception desk heading to the exit, the receptionist nods at him. "See you Mr. Hanson." Still focused on the revelations at his meeting and everything else going on around him, Dr. Du Bois momentarily forgets that HE is in fact Mr. Hanson. After a few more steps, he turns around. "Sorry. Bye sir."

Focused on the notes on his clipboard as he walks, Dr. Du Bois walks out of the building. He flips a page, then continues to look down at his notes. He stumbles on a shift in the pavement. When he looks up, to his surprise, he spots none other than Madilyn Hardwick.

She approaches the building entrance smoking a cigarette. She's alone. As she gets closer, Dr.

Du Bois' anxiety grows. Madilyn walks right past Dr. Du Bois. They make eye contact as they pass. Madilyn stops. Dr. Du Bois tenses, but continues to walk past her.

"I know you!" Madilyn exclaims. His anxiety transmutes into intensity. Dr. Du Bois takes off his glasses. He turns around and boldly stares at her directly in the eyes. "You do actually! And I, you."

Madilyn scowls at him. She walks in closer. "What the fuck are you doing here?" Dr. Du Bois stands up firmly. "I was going to ask you the same thing...though not so, crass."

He looks her squarely in the eyes, then points a rigid finger at her. "I'm researching the very reason for your visit today." Madilyn steps in closer. Dr. Du Bois stands tall and stares down at her. An intense eye to eye.

"You have no idea what the fuck you've just gotten yourself into."

"Oh, I'm well aware, and you invited me."

"Well, you've just gotten yourself deeper in this shit."

"Yep. How does my shoe feel in there?" Dr. Du Bois grinds his foot into the pavement. "Like that?"

Madilyn laughs and walks off shaking her head. She looks over her shoulder at Dr. Du Bois. "I have my reasons, for all of this." Madilyn continues toward the entrance.

Dr. Du Bois watches her intently as she walks. Madilyn turns back around with one last verbal jab. "Research. Good luck finishing that."

She takes a final puff of her cigarette, then flings the butt in his direction. Dr. Du Bois stares at her boldly and confidently. He is finally sure of himself and confronts his fear defiantly.

Dr. Du Bois watches her walk into the building and yells to her.

"Not having a spirit of vengeance, protects me."

10

RED COAT CEREMONY

An elaborate kitchen with high-end culinary equipment, suited for an executive chef, serves as a conference room this evening. Judith Du Bois, a conservatively dressed African-American woman in her 40s, sits at the head of her kitchen table. She's Dr. Du Bois' ex-wife and an Executive Chef at a high-end Atlanta restaurant. Though conservative in appearance, Judith is much more easygoing and relaxed than Dr. Du Bois.

To her side sits Dr. Du Bois and their two young daughters; both wearing glasses. Mary, the oldest daughter at seven years old sits at the table, and Elizabeth at four years old sits in Dr. Du Bois' lap. Anubis sits at Dr. Du Bois' ankles, excited.

"Take good care of my boy?" Dr. Du Bois rubs Anubis.

"Yep. He was well fed. Extra snacks in his bag for your trip," replies Judith.

Elizabeth kisses Dr. Du Bois on the cheek. "I missed you, Daddy." Mary raises her hand like a student. "Me too!" Dr. Du Bois smiles very widely. He beams.

Dr. Du Bois looks at the clock on the microwave. He kisses both his daughters. "I should get going before too dark—I mean too late."

Judith walks Dr. Du Bois and Anubis to the front door. She leans in and hugs him.

"Be safe!"

"No worries."

"And thank you for hiring the guard. The girls think they have their own Secret Service agent."

Dr. Du Bois smiles. "Take care, sweetie." He leans in to kiss Judith on the cheek, but she leans back, shaking her head negatively. Dr. Du Bois, now feeling embarrassed and awkward simply says, "OK, bye."

He makes a hasty exit.

Mounted animal carcasses line the walls along with University of Georgia memorabilia. The living room resembles a mixture of a Bass Pro Shop and a hunter's lodge. Dr. Du Bois, Dr. Fulani, and Jack sit around his living room table. Jack is burlesque with a thick Georgia accent. He's Caucasian-American and in his late 50s.

He heavy-handedly slaps Dr. Du Bois on the back. "Good to see you again, man!"

"Yeah. It's been some time."

Dr. Fulani looks around the house in curious amazement. She looks at a mounted deer head, looks at Jack, then looks at Dr. Du Bois. She's baffled by their acquaintance. She stares at them as though she's trying to solve a Hilbert equation.

"This whole mess is crazy. Still can't believe it," says Jack as he shakes his head in disbelief. He takes a large swig of his beer.

"Neither did I, initially."

"Hey, that natural pain killer you gave me, awhile back. What's it called?"

"White willow bark!"

Dr. Fulani pats Dr. Du Bois on the shoulder. "Awesome recommendation!"

"Yeah. That stuff really helped my lower back pain. My Q…"

"QL," responds Dr. Du Bois.

"Yeah! QL!"

"The active ingredient in white willow bark is salicin. Same as aspirin," adds Dr. Du Bois.

Jack takes a large swig of beer. "Never thought I'd be using herbs, but this shit work. Can even grow 'em in my backyard next to my taters and maters!" They all laugh, Jack especially.

He slides over a set of car keys on a University of Georgia keychain.

"I'll let ya'll get going before it gets too dark out. Them roads round that mountain ain't got no lights."

"Thanks, Jack."

"It's all-wheel drive so you'll be fine on them inclines."

Dr. Du Bois grabs the keys. "I really appreciate you doing this."

"No problem at all. You've took good care of me over the years, and you're the damned smartest fishing buddy I ever had."

Dr. Fulani laughs.

Jack looks at Dr. Fulani and taps her on the arm as he talks. "I mean, he will name the origin and the different species of the fucking fish we catch."

"I'm not at all surprised."

"First time I heard of a goddamn BUTTERFLY peacock bass. I thought he made that shit up! I said Jeff, stop bullshitting me."

"Look, look. Up there on the wall." Jack continues, as he points at a stuffed fish mounted on a wall.

"Nice!" says Dr. Fulani as she and Dr. Du Bois look at the stuffed fish.

"Had to get proof so people didn't think I was making shit up." Jack laughs to himself.

Dr. Du Bois and Dr. Fulani head toward the door. Jack escorts them.

"One other thing. There's a shit ton of guns at that cabin," says Jack. Dr. Du Bois and Dr. Fulani look at each other. "Feel free to use them all if needed."

Neatly manicured dense grass covers Jack's acre-wide front lawn. There's a sprawling driveway with a black Dodge Ram 3500 pickup truck parked near the house. Dr. Du Bois opens the door and helps Dr. Fulani enter. They wave at Jack as they drive off.

He waves at them, "See ya'll." He sips his beer as he watches them disappear into the dusk.

Night has fallen as they head into the mountains. The massive truck growls along a dark road with Dr. Du Bois behind the wheel. Anubis sits in the rear extension seat on full alert. Dr. Fulani rides shotgun. She rubs Anubis' head. "Good to see you, big fella."

"I figured we could use the extra security." Dr. Du Bois grabs a handful of trail mix from the console and chucks it into his mouth. Dr. Fulani does the same.

"OK. So, when I walked into his house, with all the mounted deer heads and stuffed quails...I was going to ask, how the HELL do you know Jack?" Dr. Du Bois laughs.

"Very nice guy though. Despite his demeanor, he's...tender," she adds.

"Southern hospitality at its best. He's a true southerner...and the only person I allow to call me Jeff." He laughs.

Dr. Fulani munches on trail mix as she stares out of the window. "I wish I could've been there when you met that bitch, Madilyn, though." Dr. Du Bois rolls with laughter.

"Seriously. My southern values would be exempt for a moment."

"She came off very cold and abrupt; almost brutish." Dr. Du Bois shakes his head.

As they drive along the road, Dr. Fulani's silent for a moment. The truck climbs up a winding road along a steep incline up the mountain. Dr. Du Bois focuses on the road. Dr. Fulani cozies into the seat to get some rest, lying on her side.

She stares out of her window. A tear slowly streams down her face. Another one follows. She reminisces about her "normal" and peaceful life prior to this saga. The tasks she once shunned, she now yearns for their normalcy once again in her life. Anubis moans and coddles her. Dr. Du Bois looks at her. "You awake?

Dr. Fulani pretends to sleep as she hides her slow stream of tears. Dr. Du Bois turns around to focus on the road. He puts a hand on her back and rubs it gently as he drives. He continues up the highway for a few more miles. Dr. Fulani has now fallen asleep.

Focused on the road ahead, highway hash marks zip past the driver side. His eyes get heavy. Highway hash marks start to shift toward the center of the vehicle. His eyes get heavier. Highway hash marks now zip beneath the center of the vehicle.

The car slowly drifts into the opposite lane toward the edge of the mountain. The highway hash marks are now wide right as the truck slowly drifts outside the travel lane. The rumble strips vibrate violently beneath the wheels. Dr. Du Bois jumps awake and maintains control of the vehicle. The commotion alerts both Dr. Fulani and Anubis.

"I'm OK, I'm OK," says a newly awakened Dr. Du Bois, who was momentarily not OK.

"You all right?" Dr. Fulani asks with a raspy voice. "Need me to drive?"

"No, no. I'm OK." He focuses back on the road, then peeks into the side mirror, getting back acclimated to his surroundings. He sees a vehicle in the distance behind them. He ignores it for the moment.

He makes a turn down a small road through a neighborhood. He drives a bit, then looks in the side mirror. The vehicle behind them turns as well. He has flashbacks to the moment he was followed off the highway to his house by Viktor. He starts to sweat, but doesn't panic.

He looks over at Dr. Fulani. She's dozing back off. He remains silent and does not alarm her. He drives cautiously, carefully following the GPS directions. The car still follows them. He speeds up a bit and slowly hits 90 MPH. The sound of the wind breaking the large vehicle wakes Dr. Fulani.

She looks around. "Is everything OK, Geoffrey? We're flying."

"Just trying to get there. Don't want to be driving too late."

He peeks in the rearview mirror, and appears awkward and nervous. Dr. Fulani notices and looks in her side mirror as they fly down the highway.

"Jack, he's quite the talker, huh?" Awkwardly deflecting.

"Is someone following us?"

Dr. Du Bois' poor attempt at divergence fails. He's silent for a moment.

"When will this nightmare END!!" She drops her head in her hands.

"I saw a car in the distance. I doubt it was following us—."

"JESUS!"

"—But I'm not taking any risks at this point."

He pulls his gun from under the seat and tucks it into the console next to them.

"I haven't seen the car for dozens of miles now so I don't think it was anything."

Dr. Du Bois looks into the trail mix jar. It's almost empty, so he offers it to Dr. Fulani. "No thanks."

After driving a few miles, they pass a highway sign indicating that a gas station is at the next exit.

"How we looking on gas?"

Dr. Du Bois looks at the gas meter. "Quarter of a tank."

"And there's probably not another one before we arrive; out here in the sticks."

"Precisely, and this beast is thirsty."

Dr. Fulani looks at the gas station in the distance. It appears to be newly constructed and very well lit. "Looks safe."

She looks behind them. The highway's dark and empty. They exit toward the gas station.

A few customers linger about the gas station. Dr. Du Bois visually probes each one as he waits in line. Behind him, a heavy-breathing corpulent truck driver with a long scruffy beard and shaggy hair. To his left, examining the snack rack, a woman in a greasy mechanic's uniform. As Dr. Du Bois nervously probes and peers around, the gas station merchant grows impatient.

"Next in line please!"

"Sorry, sorry."

He sits a bag of trail mix on the sales counter along with two bottles of water.

"Will that be all for you, sir?"

"Yes. I've already gotten gas."

As the gas station merchant rings him up, Dr. Du Bois casually glances at the concave security mirror above the counter. He spots a guy peeking from behind an aisle. Dr. Du Bois almost looks away, but does a double take at him. The guy conceals his identity with dark shades and an Atlanta Braves baseball cap. Dr. Du Bois stares at him discreetly trying to make out the figure. The gas station merchant bags his merchandise.

He grabs his bag, then looks back at the guy hiding in the aisle. He spots the Ukrainian flag on the guy's throat. It's Viktor.

Dr. Du Bois bolts for the door and yells, "He's got a gun!" Dr. Du Bois reaches the door just as Viktor fires two quick silenced rounds.

The first bullet strikes Dr. Du Bois in the back of the shoulder, knocking him off balance as he exits the gas station. The second bullet grazes the side of his neck.

Dr. Fulani sees the commotion and starts up the truck. She pushes the passenger door open. Dr. Du Bois runs full speed clinching his shoulder. He hops in the truck. She speeds off, burning rubber on the pavement.

Viktor runs out of the gas station, still with a slight hobble, and fires more rounds. Several bullets strike the tailgate of the truck. Dr. Fulani slams the pedal to the floor. The massive Dodge Ram dashes down the highway.

Flying at top speed, Dr. Du Bois slides around in his seat as Dr. Fulani makes hard turns. He winces as he attempts to brace himself.

"I'm OK. Just focus on driving."

"Hang in there, Geoffrey! You're putting pressure on it, right?"

Dr. Du Bois frowns and moans. "Yes." His chest and shoulder are covered in blood. Anubis licks his face. "I'm OK, boy. Just, don't jump on me." Dr. Fulani smiles through her emotional agony as she guns the truck down the highway. She looks in the mirror. There is no sign of anyone following them.

"I got a first aid kit in my luggage. Hang in there. I'll stitch you right up." Dr. Du Bois looks at his shoulder. It's covered in blood. He slowly and carefully removes his shirt from his shoulder. He observes the gunshot wound and sees what appears to be an exit wound at the front of his shoulder. Dr. Fulani takes a quick glance at the injury.

"It went through?"

"I think so." He pulls a handkerchief from his pocket and presses it over the wound. He grimaces in pain.

"And looks like flesh only; deltoid. No bone?" Dr. Fulani asks.

"No, but I sure as hell can feel it in my damn bones."

The Dodge Ram growls down the highway into the night.

11

OPERATION: HYGIEIA

Anubis guards the door like a US Marine.
The two-story cabin has a bedroom in a loft area
on the upper level. The loft bedroom is
surrounded with guns from Jack's gun locker; a
shotgun, assault rifle, and several handguns. Dr.
Du Bois wears a bandage on his neck as he lies
in the bed, lined with towels. A makeshift IV by the
bed is plugged into the median cubital vein in his
arm.

Dr. Fulani wears a handgun holstered on her
hip. She finishes the last few stitches on his
shoulder wound.

She grabs a jar of Manuka honey from the nightstand. She dips a wooden tongue depressor into the jar, then spreads a large mound over the stitches. Dr. Du Bois grunts as she spreads it on. He attempts to divert his attention from the painful situation, moving and speaking sluggishly.

"Where do you buy your Manuka honey?"

"I know a guy from New Zealand. He brings it in bulk when he returns from trips back home."

"Straight from the source. Nice."

The makeshift IV by the bed clogs up. Dr. Fulani gives it a few flicks with her finger, then it clears. She finishes dressing the shoulder wound, covering it with a bandage. "You lost a lot of blood, Geoffrey. You're gonna need to rest for a while," says Dr. Fulani. He nods affirmatively.

A cup of coffee steams on Madilyn's desk next to a donut early the following morning. She's alone and carries a conversation on her nondescript black cellphone.

"Seriously? At a goddamn gas station?" She listens for a moment, shaking her head in anger.

"This ain't fucking CRIMEA! He's getting sloppy!" She yells.

Madilyn powers off the phone, then throws it in the drawer. She slams it shut.

Back at the cabin, Dr. Fulani is in the kitchen frying up an omelet. Music blasts from her phone. Anubis sits at full attention by the stove.

She walks up the stairs to the loft bedroom carrying a meal on a tray with a bowl of fruit and a glass of orange juice. There is another small glass with various vitamins and supplements.

Dr. Du Bois appears to be in a deep sleep. Guns still surround the room.

"Geoffrey, I got you some food here." Dr. Du Bois does not respond. Dr. Fulani sits the food on the nightstand. She gives him a few nudges. Dr. Du Bois does not move. She starts to shake him frantically yelling, "Geoffrey!" Dr. Du Bois suddenly jumps out of his sleep. "What's the matter? What's wrong?"

She breathes a sigh of relief. "Don't scare me like that again."

"I'm still weak." Dr. Du Bois moves sluggishly.

"Eat this. You'll feel better."

"Thanks, Ola."

"Take these iron pills and B vitamins too."

"OK."

She helps Dr. Du Bois sit up. He moves very slowly. He takes a few small bites of food.

"So, we need to find legal counsel," says Dr. Du Bois. He pops a few pills from his pill vial.

"I know a few attorneys to reach out to." Dr. Fulani sits on the edge of the bed eating from the fruit bowl and taking notes.

"We need to move faster too. Our friend Viktor appears to be fairly omniscient."

Dr. Du Bois looks at Dr. Fulani's gun in her holster, then continues. "And our subsequent move. Massive, massive press releases. CNN, MSNBC, ABC, NBC, and even Fox News."

Dr. Fulani shakes her head. "Can't wait to see how Fox spins this one. Headline, Negro Thug Doctors...never mind." Dr. Du Bois chuckles.

"Or Bozo the Clown and his dimwit disciples will write it off as fake news." He laughs shaking his head.

Dr. Fulani laughs, "Never before has civilization been so averse to facts."

"Or intelligence, or morals, or ethics." They both laugh.

"Send this anonymously, of course," he continues.

"Would be nice if Anonymous themselves helped us."

Dr. Du Bois fervently points at Dr. Fulani. "Yes, they may help spearhead this."

"Right, especially since Justin appeared to be one of their own."

"Precisely what I was thinking."

He moans as he shifts in bed. "And they find a way to slap the hands of corrupt government officials."

Later that afternoon, Dr. Fulani sits in front of a laptop in the living room of the cabin. She types up a document with the details from their investigation of the FDA. She types like a court stenographer with her gaze locked on the screen. She takes occasional sips of tea.

Dr. Fulani reads her e-mail carefully for a few moments. She hovers the cursor over the "send" button for a moment. She finally clicks it.

She looks at a piece of paper lying next to her laptop. It's a sloppily handwritten list of Atlanta attorneys and phone numbers. Dr. Fulani starts to go down her list making phone calls.

Night has fallen in the north Georgia mountains. It's pitch black outside with the exception of speckles of moonlight shining through the densely wooded area. Dr. Du Bois, still bedridden, lies in the bed in the loft. He appears healthier and less sluggish.

A half empty wine bottle sits on a small folding table. The wine bottle label reads, "Ola Noir Vino." Dr. Du Bois and Dr. Fulani each hold a glass of wine.

"Well done, Ola!" They toast glasses.

"And your wine is delicious."

"Thank you."

Dr. Fulani turns on the television. She flips to CNN.

"Not one attorney wanted to represent us though?"

Dr. Fulani shakes her head, negatively. "They said we have no hard evidence."

"Dammit. What about your friend, Tracy?

Dr. Fulani shakes her head, negatively. "She asked me to contact her firm as soon as we locate some audio, or even pictures. Then she'll see what they can do." Dr. Du Bois looks into the distance for a moment. He takes a drink of wine. "Wait." He continues to think. He sips more wine. Dr. Fulani looks at him curiously. He slaps his forehead.

"What's the matter?"

"Justin. He set up a cloud account for my laptop."

"What? That's awesome!"

Dr. Du Bois shakes his head. "I can't believe I forgot all about that."

"I mean, we have been trying not to get killed."

He nods in agreement. "We can log-in from the laptop you picked up from your sister."

Dr. Fulani grabs her laptop and sits it on Dr. Du Bois' lap. He attempts to log-in. Password denied. "Fuck!" He tries it again. It fails again. He gives Dr. Fulani a sullen look. One more attempt. Finally, success. They breathe a sigh of relief.

He logs in and downloads the files. Dr. Du Bois lies in bed as Dr. Fulani compiles the files from the cloud account to a flash drive.

She yawns and stretches. "I'm getting to bed soon. I'm exhausted." As she shuts down the laptop a news story plays on the television.

"We have some Breaking News tonight about the missing alternative medicine doctors," says the CNN News Anchor. Dr. Fulani turns up the volume. "We just received some anonymous information possibly linking a top government official to the deaths and disappearances of those missing alternative medicine doctors." Dr. Fulani and Dr. Du Bois start yelling and celebrating.

The Zone 4 Atlanta Police Station sits with a still silence. The only sound comes from Detective Mercer's office. His desk is empty except for a copy of Dr. Du Bois' police report and a "Loss of Evidence" report signed by Officer Carlyle.

Detective Mercer looks at the documents as he attentively listens to the same news story on his radio. "Stay tuned for more details as we uncover possible links to a top government official. Again, these are unconfirmed reports at this time."

Detective Mercer spits his gum in the trash can. He jumps up from his desk, then checks to make sure his service pistol is still holstered. He grabs the Loss of Evidence report, then storms out of his office.

Madilyn smokes a cigarette as she drives her BMW X5 down the road. Chuck relaxes in the seat next to her reading the newspaper.

A phone call comes through on the Bluetooth system of her car. The name on the dashboard display reads, "Vijay Patel." Chuck looks at the name, then looks at Madilyn. He looks back at his newspaper, unconcerned. Madilyn directs the call to her cellphone. She looks at Chuck.

"Hey Vijay."

She continues. "No, I haven't. I'm driving. Why?" She gives a long pause.

"You got to be fucking kidding me?!" She exclaims.

Madilyn's silent for a moment. She takes a deep pull from her cigarette, then disconnects the call. Chuck lowers his reading glasses, and looks at his wife.

"Maddy. What's the matter, hun?" Madilyn looks at Chuck, then starts to cry heavily. Chuck places his hand over hers warmly. "It's gonna be

OK. Whatever it is. We'll work through it, OK?" Madilyn nods her head as she sobs and drives.

Detective Mercer continues to march down the hallway of the police station. He reaches a door with a nameplate reading "Officer Travis Carlyle". He barges through the door.

Officer Carlyle stands by his desk. He holds car keys in his hand. He looks at Detective Mercer inquisitively.

"What's up? Just about to head to my post."

Detective Mercer looks at the shiny Bvlgari watch. He points at it.

"Where did you get that thing?"

"What? The watch?"

Detective Mercer holds up the Loss of Evidence report. "Somebody pay you for that file from the doctor's house?"

Detective Mercer watches him keenly. Officer Carlyle appears nervous. He's shifty. They watch each other's body language. A tense silent standoff ensues like an old Western.

Flashes of gunfire exchange in the office.

Back at the cabin, there's a mini-party in the loft bedroom. Dr. Fulani and Dr. Du Bois yell with excitement.

"They actually aired our story!" exclaims Dr. Fulani.

"How'd you get them to air it with no evidence?"

She dances around the room. "I told them the hard evidence was in the possession of our legal team."

"Did you? Excellent."

Dr. Du Bois looks around the room. "Where's Anubis?"

"Probably sleeping after that steak I fed him."

"Anubis!"

There is no response. The sound of hard boots walks up the stairs. Dr. Fulani reaches for the gun on her hip.

The footsteps are revealed to be that of Viktor as he creeps from the shadows of the stairs. Just as Dr. Fulani is about to unholster her gun, Viktor points his gun at her. "Don't," as he casually shakes his head, appearing non-threatened. She slowly sits the gun on the floor, then raises her hands.

"What did you do to my dog!?"

Viktor looks at Dr. Du Bois a bit surprised by the bold outburst.

"I just put him to sleep. He will wake in about two hour."

Viktor, still with a slight limp in his walk, casually strolls up to a chair away from the bed, and takes a seat. "I would not harm animals." Dr. Fulani shakes her head. Viktor shrugs, "This is only business for me. Nothing personal." Viktor slowly crosses his leg, then rests his handgun on his knee, facing the doctors.

He looks at Dr. Fulani and Dr. Du Bois.

"Pour me a drink, please."

"We don't have any vodka, unfortunately," snides Dr. Du Bois. Viktor laughs heartily. "I want wine actually."

Dr. Fulani pours a glass of wine and brings it to Viktor. He ogles Dr. Fulani's body as she walks away, then licks his lips.

He takes a sip of wine, then casually directs the conversation with the gun as he speaks.

"You are the hardest contract I have ever had. Do you know this?"

Viktor takes another sip of wine. He savors the taste, then sniffs the glass. "This." Viktor points at the glass. "This is good wine. What is it?" Dr. Fulani nervously brings the bottle over.

"My vintage. I made it."

Viktor looks at the bottle. "Ola's Noir. Get out!"

"I fermented it from organic grapes, blackberries, and elderberries grown in my backyard."

"You make wine, you are pretty, you are doctor. I take you to Ukraine, yeah?"

Viktor smiles with a lecherous look in his eyes. Dr. Fulani attempts to hide her disgust.

Dr. Du Bois looks on, disapproving. Viktor catches him scowling in his peripheral. He points his gun at Dr. Du Bois without looking at him, then puts his finger over the trigger.

Dr. Du Bois frantically throws his hands up. "Wait! We have something you may want to hear."

Viktor looks at his watch. "You have two minutes." He sips his wine. "Go!"

Dr. Du Bois opens the laptop. He nervously tries to plug the flash drive into the USB port. His hand shakes like a Parkinson's patient. He can't plug it into the port. Dr. Fulani watches his painful attempt. She looks at Viktor.

"He needs his medication. I'll do it."

Dr. Du Bois looks at Dr. Fulani, slightly surprised. He pops two anti-anxiety pills as Dr. Fulani plugs in the flash drive.

"This better be good, whatever it is," snarls Viktor.

Dr. Fulani selects an audio file titled "MV Chicago Chat" on the flash drive. She hits play.

"What about the Russian? Heard any updates yet?" Madilyn says.

There is a pause in the recording. Dr. Fulani fast forwards a bit. Viktor scoffs. "I am from fucking Ukraine!" Viktor points at the laptop. "That was the government lady?"

Dr. Du Bois nods, affirmatively. "Yes, Madilyn." Viktor now keenly stares at the laptop. Dr. Fulani hits play to continue the audio.

"He has a few more to go. What do you propose we do when it's all done though?"
"Good question. He knows more about Operation Hygieia than he should."
"We can always hire another."
She laughs. "You're cold. I love that though."
"Was just thinking, how would Madilyn handle it?"

Dr. Fulani pauses the audio clip. A tense silence blankets the room. Viktor reaches into his leather jacket. He pulls out a cigarette and a butane lighter. He appears frustrated as he confesses. "I was only told that you were interfering. To get rid of you, so you don't interfere, you know?" Dr. Du Bois and Dr. Fulani listen.

Viktor lights the cigarette and leans back in his chair; deliberating his next move under a cloud of cigarette smoke. He thinks about his wife and his home briefly.

Dr. Fulani and Dr. Du Bois remain quiet as he processes it all. Viktor points at Dr. Du Bois.

"So, how did you get this information, when I took your laptops and your papers?"

"We uploaded it to the cloud."

Viktor looks at the window into the sky. He's puzzled. Dr. Fulani suppresses her laughter.

"Does not matter. I have new mission now," says Viktor. He shakes his head in disbelief. "They weren't even planning to pay me. After I killed seven fucking people for them, and kidnapped three." Dr. Du Bois looks at Dr. Fulani in shock.

"And that Indian. He is a fucking millionaire!" Viktor takes a deep pull from his cigarette, then mumbles a quote in Ukrainian. *"Poverty is in want of much; avarice - of everything."*

Viktor stands up and reaches into his pocket. He pulls out some dog treats in a plastic bag, then throws them to Dr. Du Bois.

"In Ukraine, my dog loves these. Made from pure beef."

Dr. Du Bois looks at them skeptically, but nods.

Viktor continues. "I should leave before he wakes. He will be pissed at me." Dr. Du Bois struggles to stand up and walks over to Viktor.

"You've made a good decision tonight."

Viktor reaches his hand out for a handshake. Dr. Du Bois looks at his hand, realizing that Viktor still controls the situation at the moment, he reluctantly decides to shake it.

"I have made plenty of bad ones as well, doctor." Viktor heads down the stairs. He stops and looks Dr. Du Bois in the eyes. "I am sorry about your cousin. He fought like a soldier. Must be in the DNA."

12

TEMPLE OF AVARICE

The sun beams brightly through the kitchen windows at Dr. Du Bois' house. The herb plants along the shelves in his kitchen appear healthy and green. Now safely back at home, the mood is upbeat. He's dressed casually in jeans and a button-up shirt, with no bowtie. He appears healthy and much more at ease. His sleeves are rolled up as he chops onions, cooking a meal for Dr. Fulani. Anubis catches up on rest in the living room, since he's been relieved of his 24-hour watch duty.

Dr. Fulani in a yellow dress, wears her matching flower in her curly afro, once again. She sits at the table sipping green tea, gazing at Dr. Du Bois in admiration.

Her phone rings. Dr. Du Bois looks at her and smiles. "Another attorney?" She shrugs, then answers the call. "Dr. Fulani." She pauses to listen. Her demeanor is now sarcastic as she continues. "So, you're interested in our case, now?" Dr. Du Bois laughs quietly at Dr. Fulani.

"We haven't settled on a law firm yet, but we'll be in touch soon." She nods affirmatively as though the caller can see her, then continues, "Yes. Just vetting a few, then I'll call back. Thanks!" Dr. Du Bois looks at her smiling. "They're aggressive now, huh?"

He shakes his head as he continues to chop onions on the counter. Dr. Fulani's phone rings again. She laughs, then sends it to voicemail. She pushes the phone aside and directs her attention to her laptop sitting at the kitchen table. She browses a few social media websites. Casually scrolling her Facebook time-line, she stops and looks at a link with a video posted by Anonymous.

The video clip thumbnail has a person clad in the familiar Guy Fawkes mask. The title reads, "Anonymous Exposes More Corrupt FDA Officials".

"Awesomeness!" She says excitedly.

"What's up?"

"Anonymous is involved now."

"Yeah, my Twitter account has been INSANE. Everyone's talking about this," he says as he now chops tomatoes.

"You got Twitter?" Dr. Fulani asks with a sarcastic look.

"Even better...I got Black Twitter." Dr. Fulani laughs. Dr. Du Bois chuckles.

She looks up at the kitchen counter, "You sure you don't want any help with the dinner?"

"Nope. You've been through enough. Just relax, queen."

Dr. Fulani smiles and blushes. The television is set to CNN in the living room. The CNN News Anchor announces, "We have more details on the missing alternative medicine doctors' case." Dr. Du Bois grabs the TV remote and turns up the volume from the kitchen.

The CNN News Anchor continues, "Three alternative medicine doctors, previously gone missing, have reportedly shown up alive. They are seeking medical treatment now." Dr. Fulani looks at Dr. Du Bois, "Viktor."

A Grady Memorial Hospital nurse carries a clipboard. She enters a patient room. Detective Mercer lies in bed with a tube in his nose. He sits up watching the same news story that Dr. Du Bois is watching.

"How you feeling Detective?" Asks the nurse.

"I've seen better...and worse days." He redirects his attention back to the TV.

"This just in. We now have confirmation of a previously unconfirmed report. We've just received an audio tape of a top FDA official carrying out plans with a pharmaceutical exec to eliminate several top alternative medicine doctors," the CNN News Anchor announces. Detective Mercer's phone rings and he answers almost immediately; his eyes still locked on the television.

"Mercer."

"Much better. Thanks."

Detective Mercer goes silent for a moment.

"Wasn't wearing a vest?" He shakes his head.

"That damn kid never listened." He hangs up the phone and sits it on the nightstand.

He grabs a pack of Nicorette gum and tosses three pieces in his mouth. He chews slowly and deliberately.

Dexter sits in a chair near Detective Mercer's hospital bed. He wears a Members Only jacket and a driver cap, as he reads a newspaper. Dexter turns out to be the "mysterious guy" that was following Dr. Du Bois and Dr. Fulani. He's a retired Atlanta Police Officer. Detective Mercer turns to him.

"Preciate you keeping them doctors safe while we investigated."

"All good. I'm retiring again...tomorrow." Dexter doesn't look up from his newspaper.

A large Uni-Ceutical Laboratories logo hangs on the east wall of Vijay's 2,000-square foot office. Decorated with white furnishings and finishes including leather sofa, sofa chairs, and white marble floors; the room beams, but it's contrasted with nervous frantic energy.

Vijay, panicked, shreds several documents in a frenzy; one after another. He grabs a small stack of stapled papers reading "OPERATION: HYGIEIA" on the cover and stuffs them into the shredder. He shoves them in too quickly, so it jams. He bangs it several times.

"Fucking SHIT!"

Sweating profusely in his suit, he shreds several more documents. A handgun sits on his desk, and a small roller bag sits by the door to his office.

He glances at his large-faced expensive watch. The second-hand tick is pronounced like a ticking time bomb. His anxiety builds with every ticking second. He shreds another stack of documents.

Viktor casually strolls into Vijay's office, dressed in a black suit with black leather gloves. He carries a briefcase in one hand, and the other a silenced handgun pointing it at Vijay as he enters. Vijay has no clue that he now shares a lone room with Viktor, as his back now faces the door.

The door creaks as Viktor discreetly closes it. Vijay looks up, but doesn't turn around; petrified with fear, his eyes are wide open.

Viktor looks at the roller bag sitting by the door as he makes his way into the office.

"Going on holiday?" Viktor inquires.

Vijay slowly turns around.

"I've made some bad decisions, Viktor. I just need to get out of town." Vijay's eyes are filled with terror.

Viktor laughs. "Bad decisions! Don't we all?" He sucks his teeth and continues. "We have to live with the consequences though, yeah?"

He slams the briefcase onto Vijay's desk, then pops it open. It's empty. Viktor points at the empty briefcase with his gun.

"Make this empty, no more."

He casually takes Vijay's gun from the desk, then holsters it behind his back.

Vijay's lip quivers out of fear. He cries and snots. Viktor laughs as he pleads.

"I was going to pay you. I'll double your fee. Just let me go, please?" Vijay starts to stand up. Viktor points the gun at his head. He sits back down with his hands raised in the air.

"The money. It's in the roller bag. Five hundred thousand dollars. That's double your fee," pleads Vijay.

Viktor walks over to the roller bag. He grabs it and sits it on the desk, then unzips it. It's filled with freshly minted stacks of cash wrapped in crisp money bands.

He pulls Vijay's gun from his holster, then walks over to him. He points the barrel to the temple of Vijay's head.

"Wait! The money's there! What else do you want?" Vijay pleads.

"The guy you hired to kill me..." Vijay stares at the floor in silence listening as tears stream down his face and nose.

"...He is my COUSIN!" Viktor yells.

"You greedy piece of shit!" He utters in Ukrainian.

With his eyes tightly shut and sealed with tears, Vijay whispers, "I'm sorry Amirah."

Viktor blasts a round into Vijay's temple. Blood splatters the white wall and white furnishings. His limp body stumbles to the floor. A burgundy pool grows beneath him. Viktor places the gun into Vijay's hand, wrapping his fingers around the butt and trigger.

Viktor casually strolls down the Uni-Ceutical Laboratories hallway pulling the roller bag and carrying his briefcase, as he nonchalantly whistles

"The Soldier's Song". He spots a fruit bowl on the receptionist's desk. He grabs an orange from the bowl, then continues on as he whistles the anthem.

Three lone items sit on Madilyn's desk; a family photo, a handgun, and a half glass of whiskey. Madilyn cries profusely as she stares at the family photo of Chuck, Maggie, and herself.

She finishes off her glass of whiskey, then picks up the handgun. She points it under her chin. Tears stream down her face. Her eyes are locked on Maggie's in the photo. Suddenly her door kicks open.

Three FBI Agents storm the room pointing handguns. The commotion startles her.

"Drop it! Drop the gun, Madilyn! NOW!"

Viktor approaches a Ticket Agent at the Hartsfield–Jackson Atlanta International Airport. He wears a blue suit, and the Ukrainian tattoo is no longer visible on his throat. He now has reddish brown hair. He hands the Ticket Agent his passport.

The Ticket Agent looks at the picture on the passport, looks up at Viktor, then looks back at the passport.

It's an Irish Passport and the name reads, "Killian Finnegan IV".

"Flying back home to Ireland, Mr. Finnegan?"

"Yes. Just here on business, ma'am." He says with a sharp Irish accent.

Several FBI Agents escort Madilyn out of her office building. Her hands are handcuffed behind her back.

Madilyn's tears have dried, and she holds her head high. The FBI Agents stuff her into an FBI vehicle.

13

HOUSE OF LIFE

The Jakehorne Alternative Medicine Center undergoes a ribbon cutting ceremony. Two years have passed since the string of "alternative medicine murders." A large group of traditional medicine doctors, alternative medicine doctors, and local Atlantans stand in front of the entrance.

Detective Mercer and Jack each hold opposite ends of a large purple ribbon. It reads, "Jakehorne Alternative Medicine Center Grand Opening."

Dr. Du Bois and Dr. Fulani stand at the center of the ribbon. He holds a large pair of ribbon cutting scissors.

Dr. Du Bois looks at Detective Mercer. They both smile. Dr. Du Bois starts the ceremony speaking into a cordless microphone.

"This alternative medicine center was built to serve the Atlanta community through alternative and naturopathic medical practices."

Dr. Du Bois peers around the crowd. He looks them directly in the eyes. He appears relaxed and confident. He points at a few doctors standing in the crowd.

"We have also formed a consortium of traditional and alternative medicine doctors to work together, to serve all of those needing medical attention." Dr. Du Bois looks at Dr. Fulani.

"We chose to dedicate this center to a special friend of ours whose young life was taken away far too soon," he continues.

Debbie Jakehorne, Justin's mother, stands behind them, teary-eyed. Dr. Du Bois looks at her and smiles warmly. Justin's cousin, Country Boy is present for her support. He consoles her with an arm around her shoulder; wearing dark shades to conceal his own tears.

"Justin Jakehorne..." Dr. Du Bois fights back tears. Dr. Fulani rubs his shoulder and kisses him on the cheek. Her eyes glaze over. She whispers, "You got this, babe." Dr. Du Bois nods and smiles. The audience claps as he continues.

"Justin Jakehorne...was an advocate for our industry and was instrumental in assisting Dr. Fulani and I in bringing closure to the awful events that took place a few years back." Dr. Du Bois looks at Dr. Fulani and hands her the microphone.

"It would be our honor, if his mother, Ms. Debbie Jakehorne, cut the ribbon on his behalf."

The crowd applauds as Debbie approaches.

ASCLEPIUS